FIRST

LIFE

Book Four in the Final Life Series

Terri ~

Here's to new beginnings!

By Rose Garcia

FIRST LIFE

Book Four in the Final Life Series

Copyright © 2018 by Rose Garcia

Published by Rose Garcia Books

ISBN-13: 978-1986149501

ISBN-10: 1986149501

ALSO BY ROSE GARCIA

THE FINAL LIFE SERIES

Final Life, Book One
Final Stand, Book Two
Final Death, Book Three
First Life, Book Four

ACKNOWLEDGMENTS

To my amazing husband and kids, to my Garcia family, to my Moriarty family, I love y'all beyond words! Thank you so much for supporting and believing in me! To Heather Neill, the most amazing writing partner anyone could ask for; and to Eva Pohler, the best signing buddy in the universe!

To the industry professionals in my life: Amber Garcia—my publicist extraordinaire; Steven Novak—the most patient cover designer on the planet, and Lorelei Follett—my super cool book formatter who didn't mind too much that I kept changing my release date (lol).

But mostly, I want to thank my reader group for being so amazing and supportive! Rose's Rebels are the BEST! In particular, Kelly Kortright and Jaci Chaney, thank you so much for taking care of the group! And where would I be without the feedback of my super talented beta readers? Thank you so much Wade Moriarty, Jaci Chaney, Kelly Kortight, and Jessica Ramirez! Honestly, I love y'all BIG TIME!

To the people who have read my books and written reviews at various media outlets and review sites, THANK YOU SO MUCH! I appreciate you more than you know! To stay in touch regarding my appearances and future releases, please subscribe to my newsletter at: www.rosegarciabooks.com/newsletter.

You'll also be able to access some deleted scenes from *Final Life* when you sign up! And for those active on social media, you can find all my social media links at the bottom of each page of my website www.rosegarciabooks.com. I'd love to stay in touch!

For my mom and dad

~DOMINIQUE~

GRADUATION. SUMMER. COLLEGE. IT HAD BEEN MONTHS since I survived the last and final attempt on my life. Standing with Trent and helping him pack for his move to Rice, I couldn't believe it all happened so fast. And yet, for me, time stood still. Everything I'd been through had frozen me in place, rooting me in fear and despair, and I had no idea if I could ever move past that feeling.

My parents, my best friend Infiniti, Jan, and Veronica were dead because of me. Farrell, my love for lifetimes, my protector for centuries, was dead, too. And then there was Fleet, Farrell's brother. I had loved him in my first life, and was even engaged to him. He had volunteered to infiltrate the Tainted in an attempt to save me, but he was too good at his job. Over time, he was thought to have really turned to the side of the Tainted, but he hadn't. He had stayed a Pure, had become instrumental in my final battle, and was still alive. I wondered where he was, but I knew

I'd never see him again. And since I didn't remember any of my past lives, I was okay with that.

Folding a pile of clothes for Trent, I started second-guessing my decision to delay college, but quickly pushed the thought aside. I was a mess, and deep down I knew I had no business going to college now. Infiniti's mom agreed. She took me in and was giving me time and space to work through things. She had even hooked me up with a nice psychologist, but so far nothing was helping. If only I could shake the guilt weighing me down, but I was beginning to think there was no escaping it. I'm responsible for too much loss, too much pain.

Perfectly in tune with my emotions, Trent lowered a stack of clothes onto his bed and pulled me in for a hug. "I'll be back every weekend. I promise."

At Rice, all freshmen were required to live on campus. Trent had no other choice but to get a dorm room, even if he didn't want one.

I returned the hug, inhaling his calming scent of clean soap that always made me feel better, then pulled away and flashed him my best smile. No way could I hold him back. Steeling my resolve, I asked, "Every weekend? Isn't that a little much?" I picked up the stack he had set down, re-folding the top shirt that slid off. "With a full-time nurse living with *Abuela*, and me working and taking online classes, you should really, you know…" Trailing off, I searched for the right way to complete my thought. "Do the whole college thing. You don't have to come back here every weekend."

He stopped me as I smoothed out the wrinkles of

the shirt. "Will you let me love you, Dominique? Is that too much to ask?"

Even though we'd grown incredibly close and he meant so much to me, I couldn't help but think I was all wrong for him, that somehow being with me had sealed his doom. I shrugged my shoulders. "I just don't want you to worry about me."

"I like worrying about you," he said with a grin before planting a quick kiss on my lips.

I went back to folding the shirt I'd been working on. "Sounds like a personal problem."

Trent muttered under his breath about how difficult I was being before we resumed packing his things. Truth is, I most definitely didn't want him to leave, and I'd do anything to have him come home every weekend, but I couldn't do that to him.

Two suit cases and three boxes later, we were finished. I dusted off my hands, feigning proud accomplishment, and ignored the lump forming in my throat. "You're all set."

"Yeah, looks like it," he said in a soft voice, the grin and playfulness completely erased.

Standing there in Trent's nearly empty room, I was transported back to that day in Elk Rapids when my parents had announced we were moving to Houston. It was a Saturday. We were sitting around the kitchen table having breakfast. The day was sunny for November, but when Mom and Dad had explained how their work required us to move thousands of miles away, a crackle of thunder rumbled outside. It was as if Mother Nature herself had picked up on my anger and joined me in my outrage. When the rain came pouring down, the heavens crying with me as I bolted upstairs to the safety of my room, I cursed my parents in my head. If only I had known then what I know now, I would've done things differently. I'd give anything to go back to that moment and make everything right. I'd hug my mom and dad, tell them how much I loved them, and explain how I understood their reason for needing to move. I'd do so much over again, but with them dead it was all too late. I shuddered as I remembered living my last soul life and defeating the evil Transhuman that had hunted me for lifetimes. Too many had died to save me. Would I ever be okay with that guilt?

Trent's touch on my arm brought me back to reality. "Hey, I'm serious about coming home every weekend."

Slipping my arms around his waist, I hugged him tight. "Don't be silly. I'll be fine."

He pulled back and cupped my face with his strong hands. "But I won't."

Staring into his sparkly blue eyes, I lost myself in him—his strength, his kindness, his heart that belonged to me. He was perfect, and he knew me better than anyone.

He brushed his lips against mine. "I love you so much, Dominique."

I had yet to say those words back, thinking the phrase would bind him to me forever and eventually lead to his death. I had settled instead on showing him how much I cared for him. Pressing my mouth against his, and melting into him completely, I kissed him long and deep. Our connection was so tender and filled with love it permeated my damaged heart, but always stopped short of mending the breaks. I was ruined. Forever. I wondered if he knew.

We parted slowly. Gazing into his dreamy eyes, I was thinking of opening up to him and telling him how much I loved him and how desperately I needed him, when his grandmother shuffled into the room.

"*Mijo*, Julio ride is here."

Trent pressed his forehead against mine and kept it there for a few seconds. "Every weekend," he whispered.

"Okay," I agreed, giving in to him.

Trent's cousin from Austin had come to help transport his things to school. Initially, when Trent and I first started talking about move-in day, I had said I'd go with them. But now that everything was happening, I didn't think I could hold it together while Trent settled into his new home away from home. Plus, too much had happened at Rice I didn't want to remember.

With the last box hauled up into the bed of the truck, and my stomach tied in knots, I struggled to find an excuse for not joining them. Walking up to Trent, I took his hand. "I can't," I said, losing my voice and unable to offer any kind of explanation. "I just—"

He squeezed my fingers, letting me off the hook. "You don't have to."

Swallowing the lump in my throat, I nodded.

"I'll text you when I get settled in," he said.

Another nod.

He swooped me up in a bear hug, kissed me, and then left.

Standing in Trent's front yard under a bright

August sun, I watched as his cousin's rumbling truck and Trent's black Camaro drove out of sight. The searing heat warmed my skin, yet my insides felt icy cold.

I was alone.

"*Mija*," Trent's grandmother called. Her eyes searched the area for me, still unable to see my aura even though my final life had been saved, further proof of how doomed I was. "Would you like to stay for dinner?"

I wiped the lone tear that trailed down my cheek. "I can't, *Abuela*. But thank you for asking."

"I understand. But please, *por favor*, come any time."

"Thank you, I will."

Back in the used sedan Ms. Clausman had bought for me because I couldn't bring myself to drive Infiniti's car, I wound my way out of Trent's neighborhood and into mine. Usually, when I drove in or out of Rolling Lakes, I avoided looking at two things: the lake and my old house. But this time, as I drove to Ms. Clausman's, my therapist's words echoed in my head: "*You need to face your pain, Dominique.*"

I rolled to a stop by the lake, turned off the engine, and sat in silence. Head down and shoulders hunched, I stared at my steering wheel. *Look.* Pain stabbed my heart. Grief wrestled my gut. *Look, dammit.*

Bringing my head up, I peered at the lake. The fountain in the middle sprayed thick streams of water into the air. The tall pines swayed with a soft breeze as they shaded the gravel walking path. The wooden bench beside the trail sat empty and alone. I thought of how I had sat at that very spot after my parents had told me how I had been hunted and killed for lifetimes. Trent had found me and taken me to his house to get out of the rain. I remembered the candle-light vigil Infiniti had planned for Veronica and how everyone had stood on the bench sharing their stories of her. I even recalled seeing the ghost of Jan that night on the path. She had risked her life trying to help me. I wondered if she'd ever appear to me again. Sometimes I wished she would; other times I prayed I'd never see anything to remind me of what I had been through.

Now look at the house.

With my gaze back on my black leather steering wheel, I didn't think I could bring myself to look at the two-story house my parents and I had called home for such a short time. Farrell lived with us to protect me. Yet nothing he or my parents did could keep me safe. Tavion had still found me and trans-ported me to the red desert where he had killed me eight times before, but this time I survived. Everyone else died.

"It's not your fault," my therapist had said when I mentioned my guilt over the deaths I claimed to cause. I told her she was wrong, but could never explain why. The story would've landed me in the psych ward. *"You have to accept what has happened and let it go, Dominique."*

"Fine!" I said out loud, as if she were in the car. Banging my hands against the steering wheel, mad at myself for being such a wimp, I turned my head ever so slowly in the direction of the house across the street from the lake. Using the breathing technique she had taught me, I inhaled for four seconds, held it deep in my lungs for seven, and then blew it out my mouth for a count of eight as I stared at the red brick structure.

My crushed heart thrummed out of control. My sweaty hands shook. I thought of everything that had happened to me in that house— my parents hovering over maps and scrolls in the study, midnight talks with Farrell in my room, Infiniti coming over with her hair always in disarray, Trent picking me up for Christmas midnight mass, and Tavion finding me and taking me. So much grief welled up inside of me I didn't even know I was crying until my vision blurred and the house became a distorted mess.

"That's enough for today," I mumbled out loud, taking on the role of therapist and giving myself permission to end my self-imposed session.

Wiping my face with my sleeve, I turned on the engine and drove to Ms. Clausman's. I trudged my emotionally drained body upstairs and stopped in front of Infiniti's door. It still had a giant purple *I* painted on it, and Ms. Clausman had left the contents inside untouched. Leaning my forehead against the wood, I drew in a deep breath of the lingering scent of incense, then slipped into my temporary room across the hall.

Lying on the floral bedspread, I stared at the empty walls. There wasn't much of me in this room— no mementos, no keepsakes, nothing to remind me of my old life. All I had was the replacement snow globe Trent had given me after our ordeal at the Boardman and a picture of us that perched on my night stand. We looked so normal and happy in the photo. We wore big smiles and our arms were wrapped around each other. Could I ever really be happy like that? Sometimes I thought I could, but most times I didn't recognize the girl in the picture.

With a sigh, my hand drifted to my neckline. I thought of the necklace Trent's grandmother had given me for Christmas. It was a cross that looked like a dagger. I still had it, but couldn't bring myself to wear it. My thoughts turned to the Petoskey stone I'd given Trent. I closed my eyes and pictured the smooth fossilized surface, regretting not knowing what had happened to the rock. Missing Trent something fierce, I brought the photo of us to my aching chest. My therapist had told me to let people into my heart and to trust again. She called it part of the healing process. If there was anyone I could do that with, it was Trent. I loved him completely.

Before I could change my mind, I pulled my phone out of my back pocket and texted him. *Hey, I love you.*

Three bubbles popped up on my screen, letting me know he was texting back. I twisted a strand of hair around my finger and waited for his response.

You home?

Yes.

Don't move.

I sat upright, staring at the screen. Was he coming over? Excitement budded inside of me. My heart raced with joy. I set the picture down and hurried downstairs. Pacing around the front door, I waited to hear the familiar rumbling of Trent's car. Twenty minutes later, the car parked outside. I calmed myself and opened the door to see Trent coming my way.

"Hey," I said. "You're—"

He planted his lips on mine and kept them there as we shuffled back into the house. He shut the door with a kick, our mouths not missing a beat, our bodies pressed together. After a solid minute of intense passion, we slowly separated. "Tell me," he panted.

Catching my breath, I stared into his stunning eyes. "I love you, Trent. With everything I am, I love you."

He traced the side of my face with his fingertips. "Forever?"

I thought of everything Trent and I had been through. He'd never let me down and had always been there for me. I placed my hand on his shirt over the spot where he had been shot. He had almost died for me, had sacrificed everything for me. I would do anything for him.

"Yes, forever."

He reached into his back pocket for his wallet. Opening it up, he took out a black velvet pouch. He brought out a thin, silver ring with two hearts joined in the middle. I let out a gasp and covered my mouth with my hands.

Holding out the ring, he said, "I will always be there for you, Dominique. When things are good and when things are bad. No matter what we may face, both now and in the future. I will love you until the day I die. This is my promise to you. Will you accept it?"

My eyes welled with tears. He was in my heart and soul, and I wanted to be with him forever. Couldn't even imagine my life without him. My hands shook as they cupped his face. I thought of the time I had kissed him good-bye in the rain when my parents, Farrell, and I had left Houston for Michigan. I had studied every inch of his perfect face because I didn't know if I'd ever see him again. I couldn't take another loss like that. "You have me, Trent. All of me. Now and forever."

He put the band on the ring finger of my right hand, sprinkled kisses all over my face and neck, told me he'd be back in a week, and then left.

For the first time in months, I could see a bright future for myself. Maybe I could forget the past after all and finally start living.

~ FLEET ~

SLAMMING THE RUSTED AX AGAINST A CHUNK OF WOOD, I split it perfectly in two and the pieces tumbled into the corresponding mounds. I scrubbed my bearded face, eyeing my handiwork, then examined the bright Michigan sun that had started to make its descent on the other side of the Boardman River. Buddy wagged his tail and came up beside me, letting me know he agreed that I should stack the chopped pieces and go in for a break.

"You think so, boy?"

He trotted around in circles. With his tongue hanging low, and his black, furry tail moving fast, he gave a low huff.

"All right."

Grabbing the handle of the ax with both hands, I flung it at a nearby tree. The metal lodged in the trunk with a thud and would stay there until I was ready to chop more wood. If I wasn't stockpiling logs for winter, I was fishing. If I wasn't fishing, I was toiling away on Richard's old jeep in the garage. Either way, I was always doing something. Helped me keep my mind off things, saved me from thinking about her and the people I'd lost.

Buddy led the way to the cabin, as if he didn't have a care in the world. Once inside, he sprawled out on the wood floor, his tummy cooler on the smooth surface than outside in the hot Michigan air. Standing at the sink, I splashed cold water on my face and toweled off my bare chest, then patted my hands on my jeans.

"So," I said to Buddy. "The usual?"

Another huff.

I filled his bowl with a heaping scoop of his favorite dog food, then made myself a ham and cheese sandwich. Sitting at the kitchen counter, I examined the open concept first floor, remembering how not long ago the walls were charred from blasts. It had taken me months to scrub away the ashy residue and paint the mess. I thought of Richard and Sue and the stand they must've made against Tavion's cronies.

"I hope they gave them hell," I said to Buddy.

They did.

My sandwich dropped from my hand. I searched for the source of the soft voice, but then stopped as I forced myself to tune it out. Dominique's final life was spared. She didn't remember any of her prior lives or that she had once loved me. Closing that chapter of my life, and finding myself completely alone, I had decided to say goodbye to the part of myself that made me a Transhuman by ignoring my abilities and blending in with the regular human population. No powers. No manipulation of energy.

No nothing. It was me, my dog, and my eventual death as my aging process started to kick in. But every now and again I'd hear that small voice.

"Leave me the hell alone," I muttered to the source, as I went to the fridge and got a beer. Popping the top, I chugged the contents and slammed the can down. Alcohol always helped, and so did activity.

"Let's get back to work," I said to Buddy.

Swing. Chop. Slice. Over and over again I worked with furious determination. I raised the ax over my head. I had agreed to infiltrate Tavion's ranks in order to save Dominique, my betrothed. I slammed the ax down with forceful anger. Over the lifetimes, she had forgotten about me, and the others thought I had really converted to Tavion's side and joined the Tainted. I picked up another piece of wood and set it on the tree stump. I had been alone with a mad man for centuries. Choking up on the handle of my tool, I thought of Tavion's sick grimace. His skeletal face. And then I thought of how he had killed Dominique eight times, and how she had fallen in love with my brother eight times. Now she was in Houston, with Trent.

With a roar, I spun around and hurled the ax. It whipped through the air and soared out of view. My chest heaving and my pulse racing, I sank to my knees. Buddy came up cautiously and nudged his wet nose against my hand. I gave him a pat.

"Sorry, Buddy," I said. "That wasn't very cool, was it?" I scratched behind his ears, then examined my supply of chopped wood. The cooler air was still a few months away. I needed at least twice as many logs to last me the winter. "I guess we need to make a run to the hardware shop for another damn ax."

Back inside, I got some cash from the stockpile in the back room, threw on a shirt, and hopped into Richard's jeep. Buddy took his usual place in the passenger seat. We lumbered out of the woodsy terrain, onto a makeshift gravel path, and finally onto the open highway. Windows rolled down, I enjoyed the breeze as we made the short drive to the hardware store. Rolling into my regular parking spot furthest away from the front door, I thought I heard the soft whisper again. Gritting my teeth, I forced the voice from my head. Satisfied I wouldn't hear it again, I said to Buddy, "Stay here, boy. I won't be long."

I hardly ventured out of the cabin, and when I did, I always hurried with my errand. The Michigan state police were still on the hunt for Hot Death for the kidnap and murder of Texas teen Infiniti Clausman. Luckily for me, with my aging accelerated, I looked much older than the alleged criminal. Entering the store, I spotted a new poster for Hot Death that included an updated picture of Infiniti. By the looks of it, it was her senior portrait. Her perfectly curled hair, thick makeup, and black shawl draped over her shoulders indicated hours of prep work. Remorse over her death cut me deep. I remembered the empty look on her face when the life left her, could still picture her limp body in that church. Damn that Tiny, she was a huge pain in the ass, but a good kid overall. She didn't deserve to be killed.

Damn straight, I didn't.

I stopped in my tracks, recognizing the voice all

too well, and waited for Infiniti to appear before my eyes. But nothing happened.

"Hey, Mr. Fleet. How ya doing?"

I turned to see Jimmy. A nice kid with an acne-laden face, he was the owner's son and couldn't have been much older than sixteen.

"Good," I said hurriedly, not wanting to waste time in the store for fear of hearing Infiniti again.

Jimmy looked around the floor. "Where's Buddy?"

"Outside waiting for me. I'm in kind of a hurry."

Jimmy nodded. "No problem. You back for another ax?"

"Yes, I am."

The kid scratched his head. "What do you do with all those axes?"

"Keep breaking them."

Jimmy smiled. "We got some new ones along the back wall, sir. Maybe one of those will last you longer."

I gave the kid a thankful nod, selected my ax, paid, and then got out of there. I needed to get back to the cabin, finish up with my wood, and have another beer. Or maybe I just needed that beer. Maybe a lot of beers.

Back home, I stomped my way to the kitchen and downed two cold ones. I wiped my mouth with my sleeve and eyed the darkening sky. Time to get busy. Outside, I got to work stacking the chopped wood in the firewood rack at the side of the house. When I finished, I found myself surrounded in total darkness. Insect chirping filled the air. A soft breeze rustled the tall pines. The smells of nature calmed me, and so did the night. It made me feel comfortable and at peace.

Buddy circled my feet, and then trotted down the path toward the river. I followed him until he stopped at the clearing with a round stone-bordered area. Buddy loved bonfires, and so did I.

"Good idea, boy." I gathered up some brush and sticks and set them inside the circle as kindling. On top of that, I placed a few logs. Taking the lighter from my back pocket, I set the brush on fire and blew until the flames caught the logs. Crackling from the wood filled the air. Tongues of fire warmed my face.

Taking a seat on the wooden rocking chair I had built, I stretched out my legs and stared up at the expansive sky. The warmth from the blaze felt good on my skin. The smell of earth and embers relaxed me. I started counting the largest stars, wondering how long it'd take me to die. Months? Years?

Hey, Fleet.

My body tensed. I sat perfectly still, then gnashed my teeth, pissed that the voice had found me again.

Fleet, please.

Ignoring the plea, I got up, kicked dirt on the fire, and marched to the cabin.

I know you can hear me.

Buddy turned his head, hearing the voice too, his ears in the radar position.

"It's nothing, boy," I said to him.

IT'S ABOUT DOMINIQUE!

I paused at the back door of the cabin for a few seconds, then jerked it open. Instead of making a beeline for the fridge, I stopped at the kitchen counter. My days of worrying over Dominique were done. Her life was saved. So why the hell would she need me? Running my fingers through my hair, I debated whether or not I should tap into my energy so I could let Infiniti fully communicate with me. Did I really need that aggravation? Pounding my fist on the counter, knowing I'd regret my decision, I concentrated on my energy source. Like a light switch turning on, pulses of electricity traveled through my body. Gray mist trickled from my fingertips. I loosed a stream of vapor into the air.

"What do you want!"

A hazy form came into view, becoming more detailed by the second. Big hair, pencil-thin legs, and a frown on her face. She put her hands on her hips and stuck her right foot out. "I see you're as grumpy as ever." She came up close, her mouth opening in astonishment. "Holy shit, you're old. And look at your beard." She eyed me up and down. "Do you have dad bod? I mean, you used to be so hot and now you're all like—"

"Cut the crap, Tiny. Speak your mind or get the hell out of here."

"Okay, geez, relax. And to clarify, you're still kinda hot, but—"

I blasted a spark at her that traveled through her ghostly form. "Enough!"

"Fine! I'm sorry!"

She noticed Buddy, commented on how cute he was, and then got to the point. "So, Jan, Abigail and I look in on Dominique from time to time, and something has happened." She waited for me to say respond, but I didn't. "You remember Jan and Abigail, right?"

I moved my finger in a circular motion, hurrying her on.

She sped up her speech. "Well, Dominique has promised herself to Trent. And according to Jan and Abigail, she marries him in the future and they have a child, and get this…the whole thing starts over." She paused for effect, her eyes growing wide. "Everything that happened to Dominique will happen to her kid. The mark. The curse. Being hunted for lifetimes. All of it."

I crossed my arms in front of my chest, trying not to be bothered by the fact that Dominique would marry Trent, and focused instead on her future child. Was it possible? Could Tavion's mark be passed down to Dominique's child somehow? And who would hunt the future child? Tavion was dead. So were Colleen, Farrell, Stone, and Jake. Who would represent the Tainted?

She waved her hand in front of my face. "Fleet, are you listening to me?"

"Yeah, I'm listening." I moved to the fridge, grabbed a beer, and sat at the kitchen table. My mind processed her unbelievable assertion. "Listen, Tiny, I see two problems here. One, how do we know this is true; and two, if it is, all she needs to do is not get pregnant." I gulped down a swig of beer. "Easy fix."

Tiny hovered across from me. "I know, I thought the same, but Jan and Abigail said they traveled through time and space and saw the whole thing. No matter what happens, even if Dominique tries to not get pregnant, she will."

Tapping the beer can on the counter, I said, "I don't believe it."

"I know. I didn't believe it either, but they showed

me. Abigail said that since it could be seen, then it was a sure thing."

I lifted an eyebrow at her, still unable to believe her claim, yet knowing full well from my lifetimes of experience that some things were unavoidable. "How did they show you?"

She drew an invisible square in the air. "They opened up a portal thingy that let me see the exact moment Dominique and Trent discovered the mark." She moved her hand to the back of her neck. Sorrow covered her face. "It was awful, Fleet."

Looking away from her, I tried not to think of how horrible the discovery must've been for Dominique. But then an even bigger concern set in. If there was a Tainted out there still pursuing Dominique and now her offspring, then humankind itself was still at risk. The Tainted hated humanity and wanted nothing more than to get rid of them all, beginning with Dominique. Was I back to square one with trying to stop the Tainted? The notion made my gut clench.

"Assuming you're correct, what can we do about it?"

Infiniti moved closer to me. "I've been thinking long and hard about that one and I have an idea. That's why I'm here."

Great, if she had an idea I knew it had to be out there. Crazy, even. But if what she said was true, I couldn't sit idly by and let Dominique's child suffer her same fate. I also couldn't let the Tainted revitalize their mission. Plus, Tiny had good intentions—always did. "Let's hear it."

She perked up with excitement. "So you know

how we traveled to the past to meet up with Professor Huxley and Trent's ancestors?"

"Yes."

"Well, what if we time traveled again? And by we, I mean you. And what if you stopped everything from the very beginning?"

The cold beer in my hand mixed with her hair-brained idea chilled me straight to the bone. Go back to the beginning? To first life? I moved away from the table and stood by the sliding glass door. Staring out at the dark night, I could barely see the silhouette of the trees that lined the path to the river. If I could go back to first life, could I stop Tavion from marking Dominique? I thought of how Dominique and I were together back then. I'd give anything to return to that time and change everything, but was it the right thing to do? And would it even work?

"Dumb idea?" Tiny stood beside me now. Her hand rested on her chin, her brow furrowed as we gazed out the glass door.

I studied the space where her reflection should've been but wasn't because she was dead. Going back would prevent so many deaths, including hers. But it might also prevent her from existing in the first place. In fact, it could create an entirely different timeline, one where none of the bullshit I had endured over the last eight lifetimes would've ever happened. I wondered if Tiny even realized the implications.

"It's not entirely dumb," I said, taking a sip of my drink.

"Really?"

"Yeah, really. But I don't know if it's possible. As a tracker I can move through time, but going back to first life is a lot of time. I don't think I have it in me to do that. In fact, I know I don't."

"Abigail, Jan, and I discussed that and we know how you can do it."

"Well, you've got it all worked out now do you?" I turned to face her straight on, interested in what she had to say. "How?"

"With Trent."

My mind processed her theory. Trent—a powerful Transhuman with Supreme abilities, and now Dominique's future husband. There was a lot about him I didn't understand, and I had seen him do things I didn't even know were possible. He most definitely had what it took to make that kind of time jump. But getting Trent's help meant taking him, too. Would he agree? And what would Dominique think about it all? Not to mention his gifts were raw and he had no idea how to control the power buried deep within him.

"I don't know, Tiny. Sounds risky."

"Fleet," she whispered. "Please. If you can stop all this from happening, I won't be killed."

"Dammit, Tiny, if we go back and change things, you might not be born at all. Don't you get that? *Everything* could change."

A shimmery tear glided down her cheek. Her shoulders slumped forward. "I know, but I'm willing to take the risk." She held up her hands. "Anything will be better than this."

I thought of how she had died in Dominique's arms in Trent's church. Deep pangs of sorrow at losing her and the others remained with me. If I could change all that, and prevent the Tainted from reassembling, then I had to try. If she was willing to take a risk, then I should too. Neither of us had anything to lose. Plus, I might even get my girl back.

I finished off my beer, went to the fridge, and got another. Popping it open and taking a gulp, I set it down and eyed Tiny. Her lip was quivering. Her eyes were glistening. I owed it to her, hell, to everyone, to try.

"Fine, I'll do it."

She perked up. "You will?"

"Yeah."

She jumped for joy. "I knew you'd help, Fleet! I knew it!"

I jabbed a finger in her direction. "Me giving it a try doesn't mean it'll work. And if I'm successful, it doesn't necessarily mean we'll get the result we want. Understand? So bring it down a notch."

My admonishment had no effect on her whatso-ever because she continued beaming with glee. "Yes, I understand."

"Now, get out of here," I commanded her with a wave. "I've got lots to do to get ready and I don't need you pestering me. I'll call you when I'm ready."

Having her convince me was probably the easy part, and she didn't even know it. Now we had to go to Dominique and Trent, explain everything, and see if they would want to take their chances on the future or risk everything and travel to the past.

Infiniti crossed her arms, but kept the grin on her face. "Always the tough guy." She drifted closer to me and laid her small hand on mine. "Thanks, Fleet."

With Infiniti gone and Buddy at my heels, I prepared for my trip to Houston. Securing the cabin and the grounds would be no big deal. The hard part would be tapping into my Transhuman abilities after letting them go dormant for so long. It would take at least a couple of months to regenerate my abilities. I spent the days outside, letting the electromagnetic radiation given off by the sun recharge me on a cellular level. At night, I cocooned myself in my energy force, resting in my own essence so my charge would continue while I slept. Once brimming with enough power, I got busy sharpening my skills.

Gathering my energy at my fingertips, I practiced chopping wood with my vaporized blasts. Over and over I split the timber with ease. Sometimes I'd use a razor-thin stream to meticulously slice the logs in half. Other times I let my blasts surge out of me with violent force, obliterating the logs into smithereens. Buddy didn't care for any of it, barking at me from afar at each blast, his agitation increasing with each day.

Powering down one day, I called him over to me. "Come here, boy."

He approached with caution, and seeing him scared like that made me feel like shit. I crouched down and scratched him behind his ears. "I'm sorry about the noise." Rubbing him down his back, I said, "I should probably find someone to take you in sooner than later."

As if understanding my words, he gave my hand a lick.

"Come on, boy. No more blasts for today. What do you say we go inside for a snack?"

He huffed at me with his tail wagging and trotted back to the cabin. I followed, wondering about what

I'd do with him. He'd been my best friend for so many months, my constant and faithful companion when I was at my lowest. I owed it to him to find him a place where he'd be safe and cared for. As I entered the house, I spotted my ax by the door and paused mid-step.

"Jimmy," I said to Buddy. "I can ask Jimmy if he'll take you."

I tossed a bone to Buddy and made myself a sandwich. "We'll go to the hardware store in the morning and ask him."

The next day was cloudy and drizzly. A sharp coolness had invaded the summer air. Taking a minute to study the sky, I realized a couple of months had passed since my discussion with Infiniti, if not more. Almost all the leaves on the trees had turned to shades of red, orange, and yellow. The multi-colored coverings littered the ground.

"You ready?" I asked Buddy.

With his tongue out, he perked his ears and tilted his head. Leaving him was not going to be easy.

"Let's get this over with, boy."

Buddy and I made our way to the hardware store in short order. Parking the car, I gave him a good rub. I hoped he wouldn't be too pissed at me for leaving him and somehow he'd know I was giving him to Jimmy for his own good.

"You'll understand, right Buddy?"

He huffed.

"Good."

Once inside, I spotted Jimmy behind the register. "Hey, Jimmy." He gave me a curious glance, but I kept on with my request before I changed my mind.

"Listen, I'm heading out of town for a few weeks, maybe longer, and need someone to take care of Buddy." I laid an envelope filled with cash on the counter and tapped it. "There's enough money here for food and treats and any other expenses. Do you think you can help me out?"

Jimmy's mouth hung open. I looked behind me to see what was up, but didn't see anything. I turned back around and snapped my fingers in front of his face. "Kid, you okay?"

"Uh...Mr. Fleet? Is that...you?"

"What?"

"You look...different."

Jimmy's gazed shifted to the wanted sign for Hot Death, and then drifted back to me. Surprise and terror had taken over his usual easygoing appearance.

"Son of a bitch," I mumbled under my breath, realizing that reclaiming my powers had reversed my aging and suddenly I was Hot Death again, complete with a young face and a recent shave. I reached over, tugged the wanted sign off the wall, and crumpled it in my hand. "This is not what it seems, Jimmy. You have to trust me."

Jimmy stayed silent.

Great, this was not at all what I had planned. Processing my situation, I knew I needed to zap my way out of there, and quick. But first, I needed to get outside. I placed my car keys on the thick packet of money. "Take the cash, my car, and take care of Buddy. Can you do that for me? Please? He's in the car outside in my regular spot."

Jimmy gulped. "Y-y-yes, sir."

I kept a slow pace as I walked out of the store,

trying not to rush out and draw attention to myself, when I heard the cocking of a rifle from behind me.

"Hands in the air, Mr. Fleet."

I recognized Jimmy's dad's voice and froze in place, cursing at myself in my head because I most definitely wasn't ready for this. How could I have been so careless? I lifted my hands.

"Down on the ground. Now."

I turned to face Jimmy's dad, my hands still up in surrender. A sprinkle of rain started to come down on me. "It's not what you think, Mr. Brown."

"You can explain that to the authorities, Hot Death. Now, on the ground."

I rubbed my fingertips together, sending out short bursts of sparks into the air. With the haze and drizzle, the flickers went unnoticed by Mr. Brown. Jimmy exited the store and stood behind his dad, his face still plastered with shocked amazement. A few curious patrons came out of the store, too. Some with their phones up and pointed at me. Was I strong enough to freeze them with my power? I hadn't practiced that yet, and wasn't sure I had it in me, but I had to try.

Mr. Brown jerked his rifle forward. "Do it."

"Okay, I'll do it," I said. With a quick flick, I flung out an explosion of gray vapor. The spray crackled in the air all about me as I lunged to the ground in case my efforts were unsuccessful. I heard the rifle and the phones clatter to the ground. I stayed on the asphalt for a few seconds, straining my ears for any other sounds, but didn't hear anything. The air had gone still.

"You did it," Tiny said, shimmering into view beside me.

I got up, dusted off my jeans, and surveyed the area. Everyone stood perfectly still. Even the cars on the road passing the store had frozen in place. I walked over to my jeep to check on Buddy. He was staring out the window, tongue hanging out, tail stopped mid-swish. I rubbed his motionless head. "I'll miss you, boy."

Cutting my good-bye short before Tiny could detect my pain; I spun around and met her eager stare. "Let's roll."

~DOMINIQUE~

PLAYING WITH THE RING ON MY FINGER, I TRIED TO READ my online Expository Writing assignment…again. I'd read it at least three times already but couldn't focus because all I could think about was Trent coming over in a few hours. True to his word, he'd been home every weekend since college started. With our relationship moving to the next level, it was getting harder and harder to be apart. I couldn't wait to see him.

Closing my laptop, I had given up on my task and flopped on my bed, when my phone rang. I looked at the screen and saw Trent was calling me, which he never did. Shooting upright, I answered quickly.

"Hey," I said.

"Dominique," he blew out. "You're okay."

My stomach tightened. "Of course, I'm okay. Why wouldn't I be?" I asked, letting out a nervous laugh.

My mind raced with different scenarios of how I might be in danger—Tavion returning from the dead, a new threat coming for me, something happening to

Trent, the end of the entire freaking world. I forced myself to stop my out-of-control thoughts like my therapist had taught me and focused on the fact that I was fine. Nothing was wrong. I glanced out the window. The sun shone with brilliant intensity, the clear blue sky gave no hint of menace. If only the long pause by Trent matched my calming efforts, but I recognized all too well the thick worry in his silence. "Trent," I half-whispered. "You're scaring me."

He finally found his voice. "Hot Death has been spotted. It's all over the news."

Tingles of panic erupted all over my body. "What? Fleet?"

"Yeah, Fleet."

I started pacing my room knowing full well if Fleet had been seen then something was way wrong. "Where?"

"In Michigan. At a hardware store near the Boardman."

"Oh my God," I muttered, my stomach plummeting as I recalled everything that had happened at the cabin by the Boardman River. Visions of death cluttered my head. Memories of pain and suffering flashed before my eyes. A flood of tears stuck in my throat. "Trent," I managed to choke out, in near panic. "I can't do it again."

"I know. And you won't. It was only a sighting. I'm on my way. Stay on the phone with me until I get there."

With Trent on the line, I initiated my calming breathing sequence. After a few times, and feeling better, I opened my laptop and searched for Hot Death. Sure enough, news stories about Fleet filled the screen. "I see the headlines," I said to Trent. "Hot Death Spotted in Michigan, Hot Death Up to His Old Tricks, Hot Death on the Run," I read out loud. My hands shook as my cursor hovered over footage of a cell phone video. "There's a video."

"Click it."

I stared at the freeze frame of Fleet in a parking lot. He was standing with his hands raised over his head. Dark features. Tall. Slender. Handsome. Deadly. Seeing him released a flood of feelings for Farrell, Fleet's look-alike brother. Farrell had been my protector for lifetimes until he had turned on me in an effort to save me from myself. Even though I only knew my love for Farrell in this life, our love had spanned eight lifetimes. Feeling guilty, especially with Trent on the phone, I ignored my emotions and clicked on the video.

"Okay, I'll do it," Fleet said calmly on the grainy clip. He moved his hands, a flash of light erupted, and then everything went black.

"What was on the video?" Trent asked.

I watched it again before answering. "Looks like someone was trying to arrest him. His hands were up in the air, and then it looks like he blasted them."

My phone beeped. A picture of Ms. Clausman appeared on my screen. "Ms. Clausman is calling."

"She must've seen the news," Trent said. "Answer it and I'll hold."

When I clicked over, I heard Ms. Clausman shouting at someone to book the flight. "Dominique?" she asked, realizing I had answered her call.

"Yes, I'm here."

"Have you seen the news? The bastard that took Infiniti from us has been seen in Michigan."

"I know. I just saw it."

"I'm booking a flight and I'll be home tomorrow. Trent's coming to see you later tonight, right?"

"He's on his way now. But I'm fine, Ms. Clausman. You don't have to come home."

"Nope, I'm coming." She shouted out more travel plans to whoever was with her. "Listen, I want you both to go to Trent's grandmother's house until I get there. Got it?"

"Got it."

"And Dominique—" She stopped. I could tell she was forcing herself to calm down. "They're going to catch that piece of shit. You hear me? He'll never hurt anyone ever again. Hot Death is as good as dead."

So many thoughts ran through my head as I considered how to respond to her, with one truth overriding all others: I was the one responsible for Infiniti's death. Not Fleet. He was innocent. But still, his appearance had to have meant something bad. Fleet was too smart to let himself be seen by chance.

"I hope so," I said, more for her and less for me, knowing something terrible was going to happen no matter what we did. "I'll see you tomorrow."

I clicked back over to Trent. "She saw the news, too. She wants us to go to *Abuela's* house until she gets home tomorrow."

Trent didn't say anything, and his silence was starting to irritate me because it wasn't helping. "What?" I asked, prodding him to say what was on his mind. "What is it?"

"Listen, Dominique," he offered. "I agree we

should go to *Abuela's*, but Fleet is not the problem. He's on our side. We can't forget that. But if Fleet is out in the open…"

"…then someone is after me again."

"No, I was gonna say it doesn't necessarily mean something bad. We can't assume the worst."

I didn't want to think about being in danger again, but I had to consider the possibility. I went downstairs and peered out the dining room blinds. "You almost here?"

"Exiting the highway now. Five more minutes."

I let out a breath. "Good."

When Trent finally arrived, he swept me into his arms and held me tight. I had never been so happy to see him, but my joy was short lived. Breaking away from him and staring into his piercing blue eyes, I said, "This is bad. Really bad."

He rubbed my shoulders. "We don't know that."

I placed my hands on top of his and stopped his movement. "Stop trying to protect me. You know I'm right."

He let out a sigh. "Maybe, but let's not get ahead of ourselves."

Sounded like a solid plan to me. Be freaked out a little, but not all the way. I could handle that. Trotting upstairs with Trent, I packed an overnight bag, and we ended up at *Abuela's* a few minutes later, right after her nurse had left for the weekend. *Abuela* had no idea what was going on, and we had decided to keep it that way. She didn't need to be troubled by the news, especially since we had no idea what it meant for Fleet to be seen.

She greeted us in the usual fashion—warm hugs

and an offer to serve us food. The menu included tortilla soup, and her homemade salsa and chips. We followed her to the kitchen where the aroma of delicious cooking filled the air.

"*Abuela*, Dominique will be staying with us tonight, if that's okay. She'll take my room and I'll take the couch. Ms. Clausman is out of town and Dominique would feel safer here."

"*¿Más seguro?*" *Abuela* rubbed her hands on the dish towel that draped her right shoulder. She shuffled over to Trent, following his voice. She held her hands out, searching for me. "Dominique? You don't feel safe, *Mija*?"

I took her warm, thick hands and gave them a squeeze. Her murky eyes settled on a spot next to me. "Well, I uh…" I paused, wondering what I should say. "I sometimes feel a little scared when I'm alone," I said, confessing the truth of how I felt, but also keeping from her that Hot Death had been spotted. She nodded, then gave me a reassuring hug. "You are welcome here. Always, *Mija*."

"Thank you, *Abuela*."

The tortilla soup was exactly what I needed— warm, savory, and comforting. While enjoying each bite of tender chicken mixed with onion and perfectly sliced thin tortilla strips, I thought of *Abuela's* meals. She cooked each one with love and care. Her feelings must have trickled into her concoctions somehow, because suddenly my fears didn't seem so overwhelming.

When we finished, *Abuela* retired to her room for the night. Trent and I started cleaning the kitchen. He filled the sink with warm water and squirted lavender-scented dish soap into the basin. He swished his hand in the water in a circle motion until suds began to form. He lowered the pile of bowls into the bubbly liquid.

"You feel scared when you're alone?" He scrubbed a bowl, rinsed it, and handed it to me.

"A little," I said, drying the dish with a dishcloth and setting it aside while he handed me another one.

"Why didn't you tell me?"

"What for?" I asked, turning the bowl in my hand while I dried the rim. "I'm the only one responsible for my well-being."

Trent dipped his hands in the water and started working on the last bowl. I could tell he was processing what I had said. "You're right, Dominique. It's up to you to take charge of your emotions and feelings. But you're not alone."

"I know I'm not."

With the bowls finished, Trent started washing the spoons. He ran the soapy sponge across the silverware, and then rinsed them. He started to hand me the cleaned utensils, but stopped short. He eyed me with concern. "You know you can tell me anything, right?"

"I know," I said.

The spoons clanked together as he set them in my towel. Part of me wanted to tell Trent about the deadly scenarios swirling around in my head, but the more I talked about stuff like that with him, the worse I felt. Of course, I didn't realize it until my therapist had pointed it out to me. Thinking about my fears and verbalizing them kept them alive, which is probably why Trent was so surprised to hear I was scared at night. I hadn't mentioned anything to him about my worries for weeks, so he probably thought I was past all that. And really, I kind of was, until now.

"What do you think is up with Fleet?" I asked, putting the dry spoons away.

Trent pulled the stopper from the sink and started wiping down the counters. Eyeing him with admiration, I watched as the muscles in his arms flexed with each swipe. "I don't know. But I do know he's on our side. We can't forget everything he did for us."

"So maybe he wants to warn us about something?"

"That, or it really was an accidental spotting."

"Accidental? That's not Fleet's style."

"I suppose you're right," he admitted.

We stood there for a few seconds, both of us caught up in our thoughts. "If I'm in trouble, Fleet will warn me. I know it. And if that's the case, we have to hope he'll get to me before…"

My voice trailed off. Who could be after me still? As far as I knew, everyone who wanted me dead had met their demise. But here I was, afraid for my life. Again. And I was tired of it.

"It's not fair," I mumbled as hot tears stung my eyes. Weary from all the pain and suffering I'd endured, I began to think my life would never be free.

Trent brought me in for a hug. He wrapped his strong arms around me tenderly. "I know it's not."

Snuggled up next to him, I told myself nothing could harm me here. For some reason, I always felt safe in Trent's tiny and humble abode. Maybe it was the display of crosses hanging in the kitchen, or the oversized portrait of Jesus that adorned the wall. I wasn't sure, but I was grateful for the peace and calm within these four walls. Breathing in the familiar and comforting scent of fresh soap from Trent eased me even more.

It's going to be okay, I told myself. *Everything will be fine.*

The soft sound of shuffling feet ended our moment. We broke away from each other as *Abuela* entered the kitchen. Her cloudy eyes gazed up a little, as if looking at something far off in the distance. Her lips were moving, but no sound came out of her mouth. She looked frightened and confused. I clutched Trent's arm, suddenly worried for his grandmother.

"She's sleepwalking," he whispered. "Her nurse said it started a couple of months ago, but has gotten worse the last week."

My life was possibly in danger again, and now Trent's intuitive grandmother was sleepwalking? It couldn't be a coincidence. "It has to mean something," I said in a low voice. "You know, since your grandmother has the ability to see auras and sense things."

Trent raised an eyebrow. He moved closer to his grandmother. "*Abuela, soy yo, Trenius*," he said in a calm voice.

She moved her hands, as if opening and closing drawers, her lips still forming inaudible words. I edged closer to Trent, starting to get a little freaked out.

"*¿Abuela, qué haces?*" Trent asked.

Trent's grandmother paused, as if she had heard Trent's words, but then kept on with her silent mumbling and moving around. She left the kitchen to head back to her room. She stopped at Trent's bedroom door and began whimpering. "*Mijo*," she pleaded between sobs. "*Por favor, vuelve si puedes. Te extraño mucho.*"

Trent latched onto my wrist and shot me a startled look.

A sprinkle of goose bumps dashed across my arms. "What did she say?"

Before he could answer, *Abuela* made a slow turn and went back to her room. She crawled into bed and let out a sigh before closing her eyes. Trent tucked her in gently. He kissed her forehead. "*Todo está bien, Abuela. Estoy aquí contigo.*"

We stood there for a few minutes, watching the steady rise and fall of her chest. Satisfied she was peacefully asleep, we tiptoed out of her room. Once in the serene beige painted living room, Trent started pacing.

"Trent, what did she say?" My stomach tied in knots as I waited for his response.

"She asked me to return and said she missed me a lot."

I drew in a breath. A hard shudder passed through my body. "What?"

"Yeah." He shoved his hands in his jean pockets, and kept circling the room.

There were a few times Trent had "disappeared" to help me in my quest for survival, but each time he had returned and was, for the most part, okay. "Maybe *Abuela* was dreaming about those times when you were away. Maybe she hasn't gotten over it."

A row of oversized windows lined the back of the

room. Trent approached the glass and stared out at the night. "I don't think so. Like you said, with what my grandmother can do, this can't be chance. Her spirit knows something is up."

I was finally getting better. Trent and I were happy. My future, for the first time in a long time, looked promising. But now with Fleet being spotted and *Abuela's* display of unusual behavior, I knew without a doubt something terrible was about to happen.

~ F L E E T ~

ZAPPING OUT OF MICHIGAN AND TO HOUSTON WAS A lot easier than I thought it'd be, until I realized I wasn't exactly in Houston. My boots sank into a soft surface, a salty breeze whipped around me. I scanned the area and quickly recognized my surroundings—Galveston, Texas. The lonely home where Dominique, Trent, Jake, and I had hid while Trent recovered from his burn loomed in the distance. From my vantage point, I could see remnants of yellow caution tape flapping around in the wind. "That's great." I kicked at a clump of sand, pissed at my efforts. "Just great!"

"Yeah, real great," Infiniti echoed.

I spun around, ready to throttle her, then remembered she was already dead. The violent wind buffeted us, yet everything about her remained static. Her hair and clothes untouched by the gusts, she could've been made of wax. "You're not helping, Tiny."

She crossed her arms, looking sheepish. "Sorry."

Staring out at the expansive ocean, I forced myself

to figure out where I had gone wrong. Sure, my skills were rusty and I had to make a quick exit from the hardware store parking lot, but how the hell did I end up at the beach? Right before the jump, I had been thinking of Dominique, hoping to lock on to her signature, but I'd ended up here instead. Probably because this was the last place I had been with her in Texas. Everything that had happened here crawled to the surface of my mind. This place was the beginning of the end.

"I know where she is," Tiny offered.

Turning to face her, I gritted my teeth. "That information would have been useful five seconds ago."

"I know, I'm sorry. I didn't think about it, and you didn't ask."

"That's the problem with you, Tiny. You don't think."

She furrowed her eyebrows and scrunched up her face. "Listen, jerk. It sucks, all of it. You lost everyone, but I did, too! I mean, look at me, I'm freakin' dead! At least you're still alive!" Her small hands clenched at her sides. "So stop being pissed at me, or the world, or whatever, because it is not cool!"

I combed my fingers through my hair and forced myself to calm down. "Back off, Tiny, before you make me say something I might regret." I started walking away from her, but came back. "And by the way, I was dying before you flitted back into my life, and happily so."

"Yeah, right," she huffed. "You looked sooo happy chopping wood and tossing your ax into the air over and over like an idiot." She waved her hands for effect.

Her description of my pissed-off-self throwing that damn ax made my blood boil, but I forced myself to ignore her because I didn't want to give her the satisfaction of getting to me. I returned my attention to the mission. "Where is Dominique?"

She pursed her lips and raised her chin. "You gonna apologize?"

The girl most definitely had a way of irritating people. To get her off my back, I uttered a swift apology.

She relaxed her body. "I apologize, too. Now, let me make sure she's still there. Hold on." She disappeared then reappeared a few seconds later. "She's at Trent's grandmother's house."

I knew exactly where Trent's grandmother lived. I pictured the modest, one-story cottage in my mind, getting a good lock on the place. "Follow me."

"Stop!" Infiniti hollered. "Shouldn't we wait for it to be dark or something? You are Hot Death and all, and the Michigan cops have probably alerted the Houston cops about you. Don't you think?"

She had a point. If Hot Death had killed Infiniti, and Hot Death had been seen, it made sense that the authorities of the town where the victim used to live would be on alert. Taking in my bearings, and satisfied no one was around and probably wouldn't be, I walked a little closer to the water and sat down. Bringing my legs up, I wrapped my arms around my knees and gazed at the roaring ocean.

Infiniti sat beside me. "So, we'll wait here until it gets dark?"

"Yes."

She started fidgeting, clearly unnerved by the

quiet. Silence was not her strong suit. "You want to talk?" she asked. "To pass the time?"

"No."

She sighed. "Okay."

We sat shrouded in silence until the sky darkened and the stars overhead sprinkled the heavens. Ready to make a move, I asked, "She still at Trent's grand-mothers?"

Infiniti vanished and came back in a blur. "Yeah, she's still there."

I got up and dusted myself off. "Let's do this."

With a clear vision of my destination, I let my pent-up energy release from my body. Weightlessness came over me, and then quickly dissipated. Back on solid ground, I found myself in front of Trent's grand-mother's front door. A host of moths danced around a flickering porch light. I started to knock, but then hesitated, worried the grandmother was still awake or others were there.

"What's the situation inside?'

Infiniti answered without having to enter the home. "The grandmother is asleep. Trent and Dominique are alone."

I tapped the door and waited. Sensing a presence on the other side, I looked down at the peephole so they'd know it was me. The door creaked open. Trent stood with eyes wide. Dominique was right behind him, covering her mouth. Her hand slid down to her throat. "Fleet?"

"Dominique. Trent," I said with a nod.

Flashes of what Dominique looked like the last time I saw her filled my mind—thin, frail, and bruised. Now standing before me, she looked amazing, as if everything that had happened to her had been erased. I hated to deliver bad news.

She sidled in front of Trent, took my arm, and pulled me in for a hug. My bond with her ran deep, but hers with me had been non-existent. She had no memory of our time together during first life. Maybe what had happened at the Boardman had rekindled something in her.

"Fleet, oh my God, I've been so worried about you," she said.

Trent closed the door behind me. He waited for Dominique to release me. When she did, he stuck his hand out. I took it with a firm clasp. "I'm glad you're okay, man," he said.

Trent was always decent and level-headed, and powerful in his own right. It made sense for Dominique to end up with him. "Thanks."

Infiniti swooped in. She jumped up and down around Dominique and Trent like a little girl on Christmas Day. She went on and on about how great they looked, how happy she was that they were together, how great it smelled in the house, and how sad she was that she was dead and couldn't eat real food. I leveled her with a stare. "You need to calm down, Tiny."

Dominique stared at the empty space where Infiniti hovered. "What? Infiniti's here?" Her eyes lit up with amazed excitement. "Infiniti?" Tears started streaming down Infiniti's sheer face. As if their emotions were connected, Dominique started crying, too. She reached out to her ghostly friend. "Infiniti, are you really here?"

Infiniti took Dominique's hand. "Yes, I'm here."

A piece of my heart broke for Infiniti, even if she was damn annoying at times. And truth be told, she had started to grow on me. She didn't deserve to die because of all this.

"She's holding your hand, Dominique," I said.

Dominique sucked in a breath, her face covered in tears as she closed her hand around Infiniti's invisible one. "Infiniti," she managed to get out. "I'm so sorry."

"Me too," Infiniti said. "But I want you to know it wasn't your fault. None of it was your fault." Infiniti eyed me so I could relay the message. "Tell her."

"She says she's sorry too, and that it's not your fault."

I didn't know what else to say, but Trent helped by bringing everyone out of the solemn moment. "Come on," he said in a hushed voice. "Let's sit down."

Passing the hallway that led to the bedrooms, Trent put his finger to his lips so we'd know to keep it down, closed the hall door, and then led us to the den. He turned off the lights save for a small lamp in the corner of the room. He took a seat on a chair while Dominique sat on the edge of the sofa closest to him. Infiniti stayed near her friend. Not wanting to sit, I took my place close to the windows.

"We saw you were spotted in Michigan," Trent said. "It's all over the social media."

"Yeah, I figured I'd make the news again and you'd see it," I said, remembering those raised phones and pissed off at myself for being careless. "That was an accident. I didn't mean to be spotted."

"You were right," Dominique said to Trent. She let out a breath of relief. Her shoulders relaxed. "It was an accident. There's nothing up."

"Well," I said, letting the word linger for a minute while I tried to think of what to say next. "Not exactly."

Trent moved closer to the edge of his seat. "What do you mean, not exactly?"

Infiniti floated closer to me. "Spit it out, like I told you. Don't beat around the bush." She started feeding me my lines. "Say that I talked to Jan and Abigail and we—"

I waved her away. "Tiny, I got this."

She lowered her head and stepped back, giving me room as I contemplated how to tell them what Infiniti had said to me back at the cabin. Trent and Dominique moved closer together. Their knees touched. They clasped hands. Pushing away a surge of jealousy, I focused on how all I wanted to do was protect her and her future child. I cleared my throat. "According to Infiniti, you two will marry and have a child. Unfortunately, Dominique's mark will pass to the child and everything that happened to Dominique will happen…" I let my thoughts stray for a second, wondering if they would have a boy or a girl. Infiniti hadn't said. "…to your offspring."

Dominique and Trent's faces froze. Silence loomed in the room like an unwanted visitor.

"No," Trent declared. "Impossible."

"Which part?" I asked, wondering if he was refer-ring to the married part, the having a kid part, or the mark being passed part.

Trent faced Dominique. "No way our future child will be marked and hunted. I refuse to believe that."

Dominique's lips parted slowly, as if she wanted to say something, but nothing came out. Her hand drifted to the back of her neck, at the spot where her mark had been placed by Tavion in first life. "But, we defeated our enemies. All of them." She looked at me for confirmation. "Right?'

"Yes, we did. But Infiniti said Jan and Abigail saw it unfold in the future. When that happens, someone will assume the role of hunter."

"We avoid it, then" Trent said. "If we do get married, we simply won't have children."

Practical and ready with an answer, I took no pleasure in proving Trent wrong. "No matter what you do, you and Dominique will have a child. Infiniti saw it. She would not have been able to see it if it wasn't certain."

"Show me," Dominique whispered. She eyed the empty space around her with a look of desperation. "I want to see it, Infiniti."

Though I didn't think it wise for Dominique to witness a scene like that, I couldn't blame her. Sometimes people needed to see things to believe them. "Can you do that?" I asked Tiny. "Can you show her?"

"No," she said. "I can't. I'm a sucky spirit ghost person. I've got no skills. I can't even communicate with my friends." She drifted around the room, then zipped to Dominique's side. "But Abigail and Jan can," she said with a hopeful grin. "Tell Dominique to focus on them. They'll come and show her like they showed me."

I approached Dominique and Trent. "Infiniti says Abigail and Jan can show you. She says for you to focus on them, and they'll come."

Trent angled toward Dominique. "Are you sure you want to do this?"

Dominique nodded her head. She tightened her grip around Trent's hand until hr knuckles went white. "I have to know."

She closed her eyes. Her lips started moving. I could tell she was repeating Jan and Abigail's names. Trent mirrored her actions, and I did the same. If Dominique wanted to know, then we needed to help her summon Jan, her wise and spiritual neighbor; and Abigail, the Transhuman girl who sacrificed herself to save Dominique.

As I concentrated on the afterworld, a soft hum filled my ears. Warmth showered my skin. I opened my eyes and saw a bright light hovering in the room. The glow grew until it took on the shape of two people—Jan and Abigail.

Jan approached Dominique with a sad look on her face. "My dear. I am pleased to see you, though wish it were under different circumstances."

"I wish, too," Abigail added in a small voice.

"Thank you both for coming," Dominique replied in a shaky voice. "I was hoping you could show me," she glanced at Trent, "us, our future child."

"The moment we discover our child's mark," Trent tacked on.

"I see," Jan said, her tone melancholy and serious. "Of course, I'll show you."

She held out her hands. A dim light formed above her palms. Using her fingers, she stretched out the light until it formed a rectangular shape, like an over-sized mirror. Within the supernatural frame, a hospital room came into focus. Balloons and flowers filled the tiny room. Blue and yellow hues dominated the color scheme.

"A boy," Dominique choked out. "We're going to have a boy."

Although Dominique was sitting up in the hospital bed, her eyes were closed. A little older and looking exhausted, she was still as beautiful as ever. Trent sat in a chair by her side, dozing off as he read a book. They appeared to be in their late twenties.

A nurse entered the room, pushing a rolling bassinet. Inside was a bundled baby. "Good morning, Mom and Dad," the nurse announced with a smile. She walked over to the window and opened the blinds. Sunlight poured into the room. "The baby is ready for a change, a feeding, and a new swaddle. I'll leave you to it, and I'll be back later."

Despite her weariness, Dominique's eyes sparkled with happiness. So did Trent's. She swung her legs off the bed. She shuffled over to the cart. Trent kept one hand on her back and the other on her elbow. Excitement, joy, and nervousness covered their faces as they began working on their son, when suddenly the mood in the room changed. Their faces dropped. Their eyes went wide. Tears welled up in Dominique's eyes. "No, no, no. It can't be," Dominique pleaded. "It can't!"

Dominique edged closer to the mystical image. "What is it?" she begged. She threw Jan a desperate look. "What are Trent and I seeing?"

Jan waved her hand. The scene zoomed in. Trent had the baby resting on his forearm while he loosened the hospital blanket. With the back of the baby's neck fully exposed, Dominique leaned in to help, when she stopped. There was a small red dot on the baby's skin, right at his hairline. She brushed her fingers over it. The mark spread at her touch, taking on the shape of a fingerprint, the exact same shape as the mark she wore.

Dominique swept the gut-wrenching scene away. Trent grabbed her shoulders. She turned into him and buried her face in the crook of his neck. "I didn't want to believe it," she sobbed.

Riveted by the sheer and utter horror of the scene, no one was able to say anything. Infiniti hovered next to me, weeping. Jan and Abigail clung to each other for comfort. After a while, Jan approached Dominique and Trent. "I am truly sorry, my dears."

"How?" Trent asked Jan with watery eyes.

Jan folded her hands before her. "It appears the mark is a part of Dominique's energy. I believe it travels with her, and is unavoidable."

The ghostly matriarch and child faded away, leaving me and Infiniti with the broken-hearted Dominique and Trent. I wanted nothing more than to take away her pain, but I felt weak and powerless. Keeping my distance, I looked away. My eyes blurred with tears. A clog of emotions stuck in my throat.

Dominique and Trent sank down to the couch. Infiniti drifted over to them and joined them in their sorrow. As always, I was the outsider, but had grown used to my position.

"There's no way to see who the hunter is?" Trent asked. He appeared equal parts despondent and furious. "Who will do this?"

"Jan and Abigail couldn't see that part," Infiniti said.

"Infiniti says Jan and Abigail couldn't see that part," I repeated.

"You came all this way to tell us of an unknown attacker?" Trent asked. "We can't do anything with that!"

Dominique looked crushed. After a while, she settled her gaze on me. "If you can't tell us who the future threat is, then why are you here?"

Finally, we were at the heart of the matter. I wondered what they'd think of the idea to return to first life and prevent Dominique from being marked by Tavion.

"I'm here to tell you the only way to prevent the future from happening is to go back to the very beginning to stop Dominique from being marked in the first place."

Every little creak from the settling house sounded amplified, as if the house itself was surprised at my suggestion.

Dominique clutched Trent's arm. "What? Go back to first life?"

"Yes. Go back and kill Tavion before he marks you. It'll create a different timeline, and it might screw up all our futures, but it'll prevent a lot of deaths," I said. "Mainly yours and your son's."

"And me," Infiniti interjected.

"And Infiniti's. Trick is, I'll need Trent's help to get there." I stopped short of telling them Trent helping me meant he'd be going too. I wanted to see their reaction to the idea itself before going into any detail.

"My parents, Farrell, Infiniti, Jan, Veronica," Dominique uttered. "None of them will have died. I will be spared, and so will our child. But we may never meet," she said to Trent, the pain etched on her beautiful face.

"And so we're clear," I added, "this is only a theory. I can go to first life with the intention of killing Tavion, but I can't guarantee I'll be successful."

"But you think you can, right?" Trent asked. "You think you can kill him?"

Years upon years of my time with that madman filled me with rage. His skeletal face, his evil mind, all the horrific things he made me do—it was all still so fresh in my mind. I could never escape my time with him. Killing him would erase all of that. "If I can get there, then hell yeah, I can kill him."

I kept quiet, letting everything sink in, realizing Trent and Dominique needed time to process. "You two talk it over," I said, making my way to the door. "Think of me when you've made a decision and I'll be here in a flash."

Without waiting for any goodbyes, I left the house. Back outside, I let the cool air fill my lungs. I waited for Infiniti to float out of the house and join me, but she never did. I couldn't blame her for wanting to stay with her friends. Zapping myself back to the beach where I could be alone, I started counting the stars. If I knew my girl like I thought I did, there'd be no way she'd pass up the chance to save so many people. And if I was right about Trent and his high moral code, he'd feel the same way. I only hoped they'd call out to me sooner than later because the only thing that could stand in our way would be the cops finding Hot Death first.

~DOMINIQUE~

EVERYTHING FLEET HAD SAID REPLAYED OVER AND OVER in my mind. Trent and I would marry, we'd have a child, and our child would be hunted. Part of me couldn't believe it, another part of me had no doubt it would happen. I was doomed, and so was everyone linked to me. My worst fears had been confirmed. There was no escaping it, but could we prevent it by traveling back to first life and killing Tavion before he could mark me? Was it really possible?

After crying out every last tear in my body, Trent and I clung to each other on the couch. We desperately held on for comfort, for understanding, and for a hope we knew didn't exist.

"We need to try," I whispered. "If we can save everyone, including our future child, then we have to do it."

"I know," he whispered back. He kissed me tenderly, our bodies melding together in an intense bond mixed with longing and sadness. "I love you so much, Dominique. No matter what happens, I will find you. In this life, in the next, in an alternate reality, I will always be with you."

My heart surged with the hope of being linked to Trent forever. We had yet to consummate our promise to each other, both of us waiting for the perfect time, but now was all we had, and I wanted him more than anything.

"I want you, Trent," I said in a soft voice. "All of you."

He studied me with his beautiful face and amazing blue eyes I always got lost in. "Are you sure?"

I traced his face with my fingers. "Yes. I'm sure."

He pulled off his shirt to expose his perfectly sculpted chest. Staring at the spot where he had been shot, I lighted my fingers on his scar. "I did that," I choked out, my voice filled with heavy remorse.

He took my hand and pressed it against his mouth. "No, you didn't," he said, kissing my fingers.

Closing my eyes, focusing on him alone, I worked my hands around his neck and brought him to me. Losing ourselves in our desire, we explored each other completely—kissing, touching, holding—our hearts exploding with love and breaking with sorrow knowing this would be our first and last time together.

———

STREAMS OF DAYLIGHT POURED INTO THE ROOM, WAKING me. I didn't feel Trent's body next to mine, so figured he'd gotten up before his grandmother could find us. Still reeling from the revelations of the night before, yet savoring the splendor of what Trent and I had shared, I got up slowly, not wanting to face the day. If only time would stand still for us.

"Hey, beautiful," Trent said. He came into the room and sat on the wooden coffee table. He held out a cup of coffee for me.

I pushed my long hair from my face and greeted him with a smile. How he was able to maintain an upbeat outlook was beyond me; but then again, Trent was always the positive one. I made a mental note to be more like him.

"Good morning," I said, taking the cup from his hand. I wrapped my hands around the mug and let it warm my palms, then inhaled the mocha-flavored goodness. I took a sip. "Mmm, delicious. Thank you. Where's *Abuela*?" I asked, not hearing her usual bustle from the kitchen.

"Sister Joanne picked her up early for an all-day church retreat. She wanted me to tell you to have a good day."

"We're alone?" I asked, thinking of the amazing things we had done the night before, and wanting to do them all over again.

His smile grew wide. "Yes."

Ah, so that explained his upbeat demeanor. Practically leaping from the couch, I gave him a quick peck on the lips before making a dash to the bathroom. With *Abuela* gone, we had all day to be together. Our troubles could wait. I brushed my teeth, washed my face, and then stared at myself in the mirror. The tender way Trent had touched me, the things he had whispered in my ear, the look on his face as we experienced each other like never before sent tingles all over me. Our night had been spontaneous and passion-filled; our emotions raw and unfiltered. I couldn't wait to do it all again.

The sound of the doorbell jolted me from my thoughts and brought me back to our grim reality. *Abuela* was gone, so we weren't expecting any visitors. I rifled through my duffle bag and put on fresh jeans and a shirt before hurrying to the front door.

Trent stood in the foyer with a man in khaki-colored pants and a black leather jacket. I recognized him as the detective who had talked to me when I had been brought home from Michigan to Texas after what I had explained as a kidnapping.

"Detective…" I paused trying to remember his name.

"Detective Rodriguez," Trent said.

"Yes, of course. Detective Rodriguez."

The man smiled. "Hello, Ms. Wells. Good to see you." He stuck his hand out and gave me a firm shake.

"How can we help you, Detective?" Trent asked.

"No cause for alarm. I came here when no one answered at Ms. Clausman's house. I'm assuming you've both heard that Hot Death has been spotted in Michigan?"

A blast of worry coursed through my body. Suddenly I wondered where Fleet was and if he was okay.

"Yes," Trent said. "We heard."

Detective Rodriguez kept quiet, as if waiting for us to say something, but I was at a loss for words.

"Dominique, you said Hot Death had nothing to do with your kidnapping, correct?"

I swallowed; scared the lies I had spun to explain my bruises and how I had ended up in Michigan would unravel somehow. "Uh, yeah, that's right."

Detective Rodriguez shifted in his boots. The sound of creaking leather filled the air. "I know you said you couldn't make out the face of your abductor, but I was wondering if anything about your ordeal has come back to you." His brown eyes stayed on me, and I felt like I was under interrogation. "Anything at all, Ms. Wells. Hot Death is still wanted for the death of your friend. With him being spotted, we don't want to leave any stone unturned."

"Detective," Trent said. "Are you saying Hot Death is connected to Dominique?"

"Is that what *you* think?" Detective Rodriguez asked.

"No," Trent replied. "Not at all. But it sure sounds like that's what *you're* saying."

Detective Rodriguez fell silent again. "Hot Death was seen very close to the spot where you kids were found in Michigan. I'm sure the connection hasn't gone unnoticed by you."

The blood drained from my face. I could even feel it pooling in my legs. "No, it hasn't."

"And you went to Ms. Wells when she broke away from her abductor and called you, correct?" Detective Rodriguez asked Trent.

"That's right," Trent confirmed.

The detective rocked back on the heels of his boots. He moved his hand to the top of the gun he wore at his hip and rested it there. His leather jacket squeaked. "Listen, Hot Death has been spotted and I want you kids to be alert."

"Yes," I said. "Of course."

He handed me and Dominique his business card. "If you see anything suspicious, or if any details about your abduction come back to you, I want you to call me right away. Sometimes memories can return over time." He shifted his attention to Trent. "That goes for you, too."

"Sure thing, Detective," Trent said.

"Absolutely," I added. "Thank you for checking on us."

"Yeah, thank you, Detective Rodriguez," Trent added.

Trent opened the door for the detective and closed it softly behind him. He looked out the peep hole, then turned to me. "As much as I want to spend the day with you, I think we need to talk to Fleet." He rubbed the back of his neck. "I'm feeling like time is not on our side."

Trent echoed my sentiments exactly. It was as if we were standing on a ticking time bomb with the countdown suddenly accelerating. We didn't know exactly how to reach out to Fleet, so decided if we both concentrated on him like he said, he'd show up. And he did. Smelling like salty air, he appeared with windblown hair and sand on his boots. I envied that he had been on the beach, and wondered if I'd ever see the ocean again.

Searching the space about him, I asked, "Is Infiniti with you?'

"No, she's not." He looked around the room. "She's not here either." I must've had a disappointed look on my face because he added, "Don't worry.

She'll show up." Then he half-muttered under his breath, "She always does."

Running his hands through his hair, Fleet asked, "Did you all decide what you want to do?"

Trent laced his fingers with mine. "We're in," he said.

"If we can save our future son and spare the deaths of so many, then we have to try," I added, forcing myself not to focus on the fact that changing things could mean I'd never meet Trent. I thought of being with Trent the night before and how we had pledged to find each other no matter what. I had no idea if a concept like that was possible, but I had to believe somehow, somewhere, Trent and I would end up together. My phone beeped. Looking at it, I saw Ms. Clausman was texting.

Flight delayed. Will be in Houston tonight. You good?
Yes, I'm good. With Trent.
Okay. Stay there. I'll text you flight info once I get it.
Ok.

"Ms. Clausman's flight is delayed. She'll be in later tonight," I said to Trent and Fleet.

"And your grandmother?" Fleet asked Trent.

"She's on a church retreat. She'll be gone all day."

"Okay, so today is the day," Fleet said, rubbing his hands together. "We can get our game plan together and then get ready for the time jump."

As if he had proclaimed our death sentence, my stomach sank. My knees weakened. I sat down, almost in shock, scared as hell at what we were about to do. Fleet moved about the room and closed the curtains and blinds. He and Trent were talking, maybe even strategizing, but I was so lost in thought I wasn't paying attention.

Settle yourself, I said to myself, filling my lungs with air. I counted to four. *Lives will be saved. Lifetimes of pain will be avoided.* After holding my breath for seven seconds, I let it trickle through my lips for a count of eight. *I can do this. I know I can.*

Feeling slightly better, I joined Trent and Fleet's conversation.

"So we link hands and concentrate on a time and place?" Trent asked.

"Yeah," Fleet said. "We'll be going to the Boardman River, which you're already familiar with, but this time we're traveling to 1868."

"The Boardman? You all lived there back then?" I asked.

"Yes," Fleet said. "That's always been our home. For the most part, it was a place away from all the fighting. A place of peace and solitude."

"1868," Trent muttered. "Three years after the end of the Civil War."

"The war was officially declared over in 1865, but it was still a time of great conflict," Fleet added. "Tavion admired the war, and not in a good way. We suspected he played a role in the uprising, but we never knew for sure. Your dad even challenged him about it, Dominique."

"My dad?" I thought of the pain I had felt when my dad was killed, could see the blood spilling through the snow when Farrell had attacked him. My heart stabbed with pain, but I pushed the memory aside. I focused on first life, curious to hear more about it since I didn't remember any of my past lives. "So I was marked in 1868?"

Fleet paced around the room, double checking the blinds and curtains. "Yes. But the details don't matter. When I get to 1868, I'll track Tavion and kill him before he gets to you. In and out. He'll never even know what hit him." He slowed his nervous pace and circled back to us. "But there's one thing I forgot to mention."

Trent furrowed his brows. "What thing?"

"When I told you I needed your help to make the time jump, I forgot to say you may have to go with me."

My gut lurched. "No!" I exclaimed, answering for Trent. "No way. Trent is *not* going." My mind had already worked to gather everything I had ever learned from the movies and TV shows I had seen where the story line included time travel. I had convinced myself that if Trent stayed, then somehow we'd stay together in some sort of lovers-linked-forever bond. But if he time jumped with Fleet, that would be impossible. I took Fleet's arm and squeezed. "There has to be a way for Trent to help you without getting himself transported."

Fleet thrummed his fingers on his legs. "You can try to break the bond with me right before the jump. If you can do it, that should keep you here," Fleet said to Trent.

Fleet's attention shifted to the space around the windows. His eyes filled with anger. "Son of a bitch," he muttered. "How long do we have?" he asked, keeping his attention on the spot.

"Is that Infiniti?" I followed Fleet's line of sight, knowing that whatever she was saying was bad news.

"It is. She says the cops are gathering outside." Fleet strode to the middle of the den. Urgency and rage flickered in his green eyes. "Time to go."

~ FLEET ~

Infiniti chewed her ghostly bottom lip as I stomped to the center of the room, barking orders. "Dominique, get to the back of the room. Trent, come with me." Trent and Dominique stayed close, neither one wanting to break from the other.

"Oh my God, Fleet, they're gearing up," Infiniti said, her translucent form alternating between being in the house and looking outside. "They're putting on vests and things."

"We gotta move," I urged Trent and Dominique. "Now."

"Yeah," Infiniti echoed. "Like, right the hell now."

Trent planted a kiss on Dominique. "I'll be right back, I promise." Letting go of her, he came over to me.

With no time to focus on anything but our mission, I gripped his hands. "Concentrate on your energy. Think of the Boardman, think of the year 1868." Standing with Trent, a Supreme Transhuman with incredible yet unharnessed abilities, I had to believe he could help me get to 1868. He kept glancing at Dominique. I gave his hands a death-grip squeeze. "Listen, man, I need you to be right here with me, got it?"

He blew out. He fixed his stare on me. "Got it."

"Good. Help me get there, and I'll get the job done."

"And I'll break our connection right before you time jump."

"Exactly."

"I can do that," Trent muttered.

I had no idea if he could do it or not, but it didn't matter. We needed to act. With my face cast down, I closed my eyes and pictured the Boardman River area in my mind. Back in 1868 we lived in small, simple cabins—Stone and Caris, Dominique's parents, were in one cabin with Dominique. My brother Farrell and I were in another. There was also a third cabin for visitors. Traveling to a time and space I inhabited would merge my current self to my other self. All I needed to do when I arrived was find Tavion and kill him.

"They're coming to the door!" Infiniti cried out in a panic.

Commanding my power to flow from me, I kept the cabins, the woods, and the river clear in my mind. "Go there," I whispered.

My skin warmed. My insides tingled. Opening my eyes, I saw shades of gray and blue energy swirling about the room. The vapors crackled with sparks. Heat started filling my airways. It was working.

"They're ready to kick the door down!" Infiniti screamed.

Dominique held up her hands, protecting herself

from the tornadic activity in the house, her hair whipping wildly about her face. Infiniti dodged from inside to outside, giving a play-by-play account of how the police were about to bust in. Trent's body shone as bright as a blue-bathed sun. I could barely look at him.

"1868! The Boardman!" I hollered to Trent. A surge of weightlessness took over me. My body lifted off the ground. Seconds away from the time jump, I tried to yank my hands from Trent's, but couldn't break away. His hold was iron-clad. If he had any chance of staying in this time, he needed to release me before it was too late.

"Trent! Let go!"

In flashes of energy-filled chaos, a host of cops charged into the house. Trent turned to face them. "Get back," he said in an eerily calm voice.

The cops slammed up against the ceiling and stuck there, like sticky rubber toys. Their weapons clunked to the ground. Infiniti shrieked. Dominique lunged for Trent. Everything went black.

MY BODY CRASHED TO THE GROUND. NOT THE WOOD-floor surface of Trent's grandmother's house, but a surface of dirt and leaves. Grit rubbed against my chin and face. Spitting out the bits of dirt that had seeped into my mouth, I got up and dusted myself off. Trent stood to my right, dazed, staring at his hands. "I couldn't let go," he muttered.

Dominique was by his side, appearing equally stunned. "I tried to pull you."

A black horse broke through the nearby brush. Farrell was on the steed. He pointed his colt revolver in our direction, then lowered it when he recognized me. "Brother, I saw the flashes. What are—" Noticing Trent, he raised his revolver again. "Who is this stranger?"

"Farrell, stop!" I commanded, raising my hand. Edging my way in front of Trent, I kept my hand up, ready to blast Farrell if necessary.

Farrell kept a protective eye on me and for the first time in a long while I remembered my bond with my brother. In first life, Farrell and I were tight. We trusted each other implicitly and had each other's backs. In this life, he had never betrayed me.

"Why is he dressed like that?" Farrell asked me.

Dominique and I wore the attire for the time—she had on a white work dress. I wore dark pants and a white long-sleeved shirt. Trent, on the other hand, still had on jeans and a t-shirt.

"He, uh," I paused trying to figure out what to say. Dominique and I had taken on the forms from our time like I thought we would, but Trent was not alive now so he was still the Trent from the twenty-first century. "He's not from here."

Another horse burst onto the scene and skidded to a stop before us. It was Stone, pistol at the ready. Dominique let out a gasp when she saw her dad. The last time she had seen him, he had been killed. Quickly taking in the scene, he kept his weapon at the ready.

"Stone, Farrell," I said calmly. "This is Trent Avila."

"He's not from here," Farrell said to Stone, pistol

still aimed at Trent. And why wouldn't Farrell be wary? Trent looked like he didn't belong here. Plus, I knew Farrell well enough to know he was only trying to protect me and Dominique.

"D-d-dad," Dominique said in a stunned voice. "It's you."

"Please, Stone," I interjected, deflecting attention from Dominique's surprised reaction at seeing her dad alive. "Lower your weapons. We're all friends here."

Stone holstered his pistol. He dismounted and came up close. I moved in, unable to read Stone's next move, but prepared to strike if needed.

"Daughter," he said. "Is all well with you?"

Shit, Dominique needed to keep her cool, but could she?

She cleared her throat. "Yes, I'm fine. You startled me."

Accepting her answer, Stone directed his attention to Trent. "Where are you from, Trent Avila? Your dress is odd, and your skin coloring is not like most in this area."

Trent stood tall. He clenched his fists at his sides. "I'm from Texas."

"Texas?" Stone asked, surprised and maybe even a little impressed. "The events of your region are rich with conflict, and tales of the battles there have spread far and wide." Stone studied Trent. "Are you Mexican?"

Memories of Tavion wanting to travel to Texas filled my mind. I remembered how he had wanted to take part in the battle to defend the Alamo, but Stone had dissuaded him, convinced that Transhumans should stay out of the shaping of young America. I wondered where Tavion was now.

Trent stared Stone down, unafraid of him and his intimidating ways. "I'm Mexican-American. I was born and raised in Texas."

Stone's eyes narrowed a bit as he continued to study Trent. "You may all go to hell, and I will go to Texas," Stone said, quoting Davy Crockett.

"Remember the Alamo," Trent replied in turn.

"Indeed, remember the Alamo," Stone repeated, keeping a keen eye on Trent. After a few moments, he relaxed his stance and smiled. He patted Trent on the back. "Welcome to Michigan, Trent. Any friend of my daughter's and her betrothed is a friend to us all, notwithstanding the unconventional attire. And please, pardon my impoliteness. These are dangerous times filled with unscrupulous people."

Trent forced a smiled back. "No worries."

"Perhaps you can join us for supper? I would relish the opportunity to hear of your life in Texas and the events that have brought you north." Stone climbed back on his horse. "Will that be acceptable?"

"Sure," Trent said. "Why not."

"Excellent," Stone said. "Dominique, Fleet, I will see you back at the compound. Farrell, you are with me."

Farrell gave Trent a welcome handshake, then got back on his horse and took off behind Stone. I motioned for Dominique and Trent to stay quiet until they were well out of sight.

"Son of a bitch," I muttered when the coast was clear.

Dominique had gone pale. She twisted her hands together tight. "I wasn't prepared to see my dad."

Infiniti shimmered into view. "Y'all are so screwed," she whistled. "Screwed and looking like actors in a civil war re-enactment group. Those clothes can't be comfortable."

"Dammit, Tiny. Not now," I said, waving her quiet.

"Infiniti made the jump?" Dominique asked with a hopeful look.

"Yes," I said. "She did." I walked about the woodsy area, kicking at the multi-colored autumn leaves, trying to think of what we should do. Last time I was here was with Buddy. The area was thick with tall trees. Now, everything looked flat and sparse. I thought of Jimmy and hoped he was taking care of Buddy. Man, I missed that dog.

"What are we going to do?" Trent asked. "What's our plan?"

A soft breeze swept through, blowing the leaves about and sending a chill through my body. The sun was close to the horizon, and the sky would be dark soon. I was pretty sure Trent would've ended up here with me anyway. However, I hadn't counted on having Dominique with us. Her presence complicated things, but it didn't change the mission. The mission… Had we even arrived in time to prevent Dominique from being marked? There was only one way to know for sure.

"The back of your neck," I said to Dominique.

Dominique's hand went to the spot. "That's right. My mark." She pulled her long hair to the side and stood in front of Trent. "Is it there?"

Trent eyed the area. He blew out a sigh of relief. "It's gone."

"Good," I said, getting back to business. "We're in time. I say we stick with the plan. I find and kill Tavion. We'll need to blend in, though, until I can complete the task."

A hush fell over us as everyone considered the idea of blending in.

"That's gonna be hard," Infiniti said.

I ignored Infiniti's comment, waiting for Dominique and Trent to say something, yet knew she was right. Pretending like we belonged here would be no easy task. I kept that realization to myself because there was nothing we could do about it.

"Okay," Dominique said with renewed resolve. "We decided to end this, so let's end it. Once and for all. But our mission is now two-fold. Take out Tavion and get back home."

Trent nodded. "Agreed. We go back to the compound, have dinner, act like we're from this time, and then you kill Tavion. After that, we re-group and return to our time."

For once, the idea of us being here at the same time made sense. Since we were together, maybe we could get home together. Maybe all hope was not lost. "I think we can make that work. I'll have to find him first, though. He doesn't live with us."

"That shouldn't take long, right?" Trent asked. "Finding him?"

"Shouldn't."

Trent took Dominique's hand. "Good. You find and kill Tavion while we blend. We can do that."

"Yeah," Dominique said, echoing his sentiment. "We can do it."

I wondered if they fully grasped what it would mean to pretend like we're from this time. In this life, Dominique and I were in love and engaged. The whole idea of being close to her should've excited me, but it didn't. She had no memory of me or the love we had shared. Asking her to fake a relationship with me would probably be like torture for her.

Dominique's thoughts must've mirrored my own. "You pretend like you're a traveler from Texas," she said to Trent. "And Fleet and I will pretend like we're…together." Hesitation rang in her voice as the full realization of the roles we'd have to play set in.

"Pfft," I said, letting her off the hook and doing my best to hide the sting. "I'm the expert at pretending, remember? All you have to do is follow my lead. I promise to make everything as painless as possible for you." I started walking toward our camp. "Come on," I said. "Let's get this over with."

I'd have to move closer to Dominique and hold her hand once we got near the cabins, but for now I kept a steady pace in front so I could think. *Blend in. Find Tavion. Kill him.* I said to myself over and over. *No problem.*

~DOMINIQUE~

PULLING THE ITCHY COTTON FABRIC AWAY FROM MY neck, I thought of our messed up situation. Fleet was supposed to have time jumped alone to first life and killed Tavion quick and easy. Now that Trent and I were with him, everything would be much more difficult, including walking. Trudging through the grassy area with a long skirt and clunky boots made every step cumbersome. An entire layer of ruffled and billowy clothing piled under my dress. Eyeing Trent's jeans, I wished to be back in mine.

"I'm so uncomfortable in this," I whispered to Trent.

"What we're wearing is the least of our problems."

"I know. You're right." I thought of Farrell and how amazing he looked with his chiseled features and his golden-hued hair. I was solidly with Trent now, but couldn't forget my time with Farrell. Could I pull off a fake relationship with Fleet? Ignore my once strong feelings for Farrell? I felt awful even thinking about Farrell, and forced myself to stop. Trent was the only one for me. My thoughts then went to my parents. I had almost lost it when I saw my dad. Could I keep it together when I saw my mom? I wasn't sure. Taking Trent's hand, I quickened my pace so we could get closer to Fleet.

"Shouldn't we get details on everyone in this timeline? Figure out what everyone is like so Trent and I know how to act?"

Fleet slowed down. "Speak as little as possible, keep to yourselves. As for the others, all you need to know is that you and I are engaged. Farrell and I are close. Caris and Stone are together. As for Tavion, your uncle has always been in a state of unrest, and it's not only because Caris chose Stone over him. It's everything about him. Tavion yearns for conflict, is always itching to start trouble. His evil streak has always been a part of him."

"Why didn't you all separate from him earlier, then?" Trent asked. "If he's such an evil person?"

Fleet stopped and faced us. "I suggested that once, but Stone wouldn't have it. He said Tavion was family, and he couldn't turn his back on his brother. But then Tavion left out of the blue one day. He couldn't hide his dark side any longer. His murderous ways and his jealousy of Stone drove him to form the Tainted and later mark and kill Dominique. There's no understanding hatred like that."

Fleet started walking again. Filing in behind him, my hand went to the back of my neck. With the mark gone, I felt better. Even though we were in a different time and place, I was hopeful for the first time that we could make things right. What that meant for me and Trent, I had no idea, yet I still clung on to the hope we'd end up together. Catching the scent of fire, I slowed my pace. Not too far ahead, I spotted a trail of smoke. With the sun almost gone and the temperature plummeting, I longed for warmth.

"Is that where we live?" I asked.

"Yeah," Fleet said. "We're close enough we should get into character in case we're seen."

The idea of pretending to be with Fleet took a backseat to the apprehension and nervousness building inside of me at being with my parents. My heart hammered against my chest. Their deaths were on me, and I still hadn't gotten over that. Probably never would. I missed them so much. I had already seen my dad, ever so briefly, and he looked the same. Would my mom look the same as well? And how would they act?

"Speaking of character," Trent said. "How are we gonna explain who I am?"

"I've been thinking about that," Fleet answered. "We can say we met in town and became friends and when your people went back to Texas you sought me out for a place to stay."

Trent nodded his assent. "Sounds believable enough." He fixed his eyes on me. "I guess this is where I turn you over to Fleet." He squeezed my hand tight.

"Yeah, I guess so."

Trent brought me in for a hug. I held on tight, burying my head in the crook of his neck, taking in his soapy scent and kissing his soft skin.

"I won't be far," he whispered in my ear.

Forcing away the lump in my throat I said, "Okay."

Parting from him slowly, I walked over to Fleet.

"Take care of my girl," Trent said to Fleet.

"Of course," Fleet responded. He gave Trent a thoughtful look. "I'd never let anything happen to her. Ever."

"I'm not going to let anything happen to me either," I said, claiming responsibility over my own destiny. I knew Fleet meant well, but despite everything we had been through, he was still a stranger to me.

Approaching what Fleet had described as the compound, I became keenly aware of the feel of Fleet's hand. While Trent's touch was firm, yet soft and soothing, Fleet's was altogether different. Sturdy and rough, his palms were lined with calluses. I wondered what kind of work he'd been doing to make his hands so coarse. With each step closer to our destination, I thought of how my fate, and even Trent's, now depended entirely on him. I hoped he could find Tavion, and quick.

"There it is," Fleet announced.

A clearing came into view, revealing three small and simple cabins. They reminded me of cottages from a fairytale—cozy and quaint. I even pictured bluebirds singing in the windows. Set up in a semi-circle, they nestled closely together, appearing identical. Door in the middle. Two windows on either side. Eyeing the slanted rooftops, they sported narrow chimneys toward the rear.

"It looks straight out of a book," I marveled, thinking things here couldn't be too bad.

The fire we had been tracking came from a large bonfire burning in the middle of the open space before the homes. Horses and a few cows grazed peacefully nearby. Chickens scurried about. Maybe my worry about being here was for nothing.

"This is our first home," Fleet said. "Life here was peaceful and uncomplicated, until Tavion changed everything."

Stones circled the wide bonfire. A metal structure straddled the flames, like a tri-pod. A black pot hung down from the center. A woman came out of the middle cabin and started bustling about. I recognized her right away. "Mom," I whispered.

My heart nearly stopped. Goose bumps dashed across my body. Seeing her alive brought a lump to my throat. Dropping Fleet's hand, I started walking toward her. My pulse raced with each step. My heart beating so hard I could feel it thumping against the undershirt beneath my dress. This life, first life, is when everything changed for us. What were we like before I was hunted? Dad came out of the same cabin where my mom had emerged from seconds earlier. He spotted us, and gave a casual wave. Mom waved, too. Farrell joined them.

"This is so weird," I whispered.

Fleet's hand brushed against mine. "You have no idea."

"Anyone else have a bad feeling?" Trent asked, his words laced with worry.

Fleet tugged on my sleeve to slow me down. "You have a bad feeling?" he asked Trent.

"Yeah, I do," Trent answered.

Fully stopped now, I let Trent's words sink in. He and his family had the ability to sense things. If Trent thought something was up, then something was most definitely up.

"Tavion?" I asked.

Fleet's keen eye swept the area. He drew in a deep breath, as if testing the air. "No, it's not Tavion. I'd sense him if he were near."

My thumb found a ring on the finger of my right hand and spun the band. Raising my arm, I studied the silver circle with connecting hearts. "I have a ring?"

Trent gave me a puzzled look. "Huh?"

I dropped my hand, suddenly remembering it was Trent's token of promise to me. "Nothing," I mumbled, feeling embarrassed that it had slipped my mind. I must've been more freaked out than I thought. I brushed off my absentmindedness as stress, when something else occurred to me. "Wait a minute. How did this ring cross over?"

Fleet took my hand and ran his finger across the band. "I don't know," he said, looking from me to Trent. He lowered my hand, and for the first time I saw a flash of worry on his face. "Let's keep going," he said. "Trent, stay close."

Walking between the two most powerful people I knew, I should have felt safe, but I didn't. Instinctively, I started to reach for Trent, but then stopped myself. Pretending not to have feelings for him was going to be hard, if not impossible. I took Fleet's hand instead. *It's going to be okay*, I said to myself. *This is my home. I'm safe here.*

Mom moved closer to Dad as we approached. Farrell stood beside them. They looked like a welcome party, lined up for a greeting, and for some reason I thought them gathering like that a bit odd. Maybe they didn't have visitors often. About ten feet out, I lifted my hand and smiled.

Mom and Dad unfurled a blast of energy at us. Farrell joined their onslaught. Their deadly streams skimmed past me. The blazing heat brushed against my face. The torrents slammed into Trent's chest. He flew through the air and crashed to the ground. The sizzlers pinned him down and laced around his body like an electrified rope.

Dad rushed over to me and Fleet. "Are you okay?"

"Dad! What are you doing?" I hurried to Trent and dropped to my knees, staring at the radiating lines that crisscrossed his body. "Are you crazy? Let him go!"

Trent's head jerked back. The veins in his neck popped out. "You're killing him!" I hollered.

"He is not who he says he is," Stone warned, staring at the writhing Trent.

Fleet grasped Farrell's arm and jerked. "He's with us. I told you."

Confusion darted across Farrell's face. "Brother," he said, almost hurt and not understanding Fleet. "He carries the signature of a Transhuman. Did you not recognize it?"

"What?" Fleet asked.

We were not prepared for Trent's identity to be uncovered, or for him to be put at risk. Panic soared through my veins. I scrambled to find an explanation for who he was. "So what if he's a Transhuman? He's our friend!"

"Dominique is right," Fleet urged. "We met him in town. He's a traveler, and a friend."

"He is not one of us," Mom warned. "And if he is not one of us, then he is one of them." She kneeled next to Trent and placed her hand on his head. A silver vapor swirled out of her hands and covered Trent's head and face like a sheer scarf. His face relaxed and his eyes closed, as if he had fallen asleep, yet the deadly tendrils remained tight around his body. "Farrell, Fleet, take him to the hut."

"I'll do as you say, but you're making a grave mistake," Fleet said.

"We shall see," Stone said.

Fleet and Farrell lifted Trent and started hauling his limp body away. I thought of everything that had happened to Trent since getting involved with me—getting shot and left in the past, having his face burned to a crisp, and now this. Suddenly, the fairy-tale cottages had transformed to evil abodes, complete with a torture chamber somewhere on the premises. What more would Trent have to endure before this was all over? What had we gotten ourselves into?

~ FLEET ~

"Since when did we start attacking innocent travelers?" I asked Farrell as we carried Trent to a small cabin behind the main houses, a cabin that wasn't there in the original first life. He ignored me, yet kept a puzzled expression on his face. "This isn't right, Farrell."

"You are correct," Farrell answered. "Something is most definitely not right."

Shit, I thought to myself, my mind scrambling. Did we attack innocent travelers in this time? Was this normal and I was the one acting out of sorts? I decided to hold my tongue and not say anything else until I could get back to Dominique. There had to be a way to figure out what was going on without giving away our identities.

We eased Trent into the small hut and placed him on a cot. Unable to do anything to help Trent, I followed Farrell back to the others.

"You've made a big mistake," I said to

Dominique's parents. "The person you assaulted is a friend."

I reached for Dominique and brought her closer to me because suddenly I couldn't trust Caris, Stone, or Farrell anymore. The whole freakin' world had turned upside down, our travel to the past clearly changing everything. "Is this related to Tavion?"

"What?" Stone asked, looking taken aback. "Tavion?"

"Yeah, you know, Tavion. Is attacking the innocent traveler related to Tavion somehow?" I asked again, as casually as possible, knowing I probably shouldn't have brought up Tavion's name by the look on Stone's face, but it was too late.

Stone kept silent for a few seconds. He threw Caris a look before he answered. "How can this be related to my brother Tavion if he is long dead?"

"He's...dead?" Dominique asked. She rephrased her statement quickly, trying to cover her surprise. "I mean, that's right. He's dead."

My gut clenched as if I had been sucker punched. My mind reeled. In this time Tavion had split off from us, formed the Tainted, and marked Dominique in a jealous rage to get back at Stone. So if he was dead, who was the leader of the Tainted? I kept my mouth shut, afraid to say anything else. I took Dominique's hand and gave a soft squeeze, signaling her to follow my lead.

"Of course he's dead," I said. "I was only testing you all because you're acting very strange," I said, trying to deflect suspicion from me and cast it back on them. "We don't attack friends. And I tell you, Trent is a friend."

"It's true," Dominique chimed in, her body now so close to mine I could feel her shivering. I wondered if it was because of her worry for Trent or the cold from the setting sun. The last remaining bits of sunlight had almost faded from the sky, its final hues casting streaks of orange and red along the horizon.

"Dominique, Fleet, we believe you, but with the state of unrest in the area and amongst our kind, we cannot be too careful," Stone said. "Your friend's sudden appearance did not sit well with us, especially since visitors are always announced before entry into our zone. You did not follow protocol."

"Trent's fine," Infiniti said, appearing in the area. "He's still restrained with all that electricity stuff, and he's asleep."

Not letting on that I had seen and heard Infiniti, my mind sorted through what I could gather as our new norm in this time. Tavion was dead, so someone else was the leader of the Tainted. The Tainted and Pures were still at odds, and Caris and Stone had set us up in some sort of recognized zone. In the original first life, we had no zone.

"We would've announced him had we known he was coming," I said without missing a beat. "And as far as we can tell, he is no threat."

"Are you sure about that?" Stone asked.

"We have no reason to suspect otherwise," I added.

"Fine, we will test him in the morning," Stone declared. "But for now, let us sit by the fire and have some supper."

We sat around the warm flames while Stone and Caris served us bowls of stew. There were no further questions about Trent, and I had decided not to bring it up again. It would've raised even more suspicion to keep defending him, so I kept quiet on the outside while on the inside I pondered our predicament. Everything was wrong, and I had to figure out a way to fix things before they got worse.

Muddling through small talk about the day, Stone turned the conversation to the river and a dam that had been built a year prior. I remembered the construction of the dam well and how Stone lamented the event, calling it the demise of the natural habitat in the region. Stone had even talked about leaving the area and finding a new place to settle further north. Sitting around the blaze, I could see that the dam and the notion of moving remained a hot topic for him. At least, with this fact remaining the same, I was able to join in the conversation in a meaningful way, with Dominique chiming in now and again. But for the most part, my mind stayed on Trent and how we could help him.

With Tavion dead and us not knowing who our target was anymore, we needed to regroup and come up with a new course of action as soon as possible. We also needed to figure out how to handle the suspicion of Trent being a Transhuman. But then another thought crossed my mind. Our friend Jake wasn't here. I wondered where he was.

"Brother," Farrell said, pulling me away from my thoughts. "You ready to tend to the horses?"

In the original first life, Farrell and I saw to the horses every night. Tying them up for their safety, it was our evening ritual and a time for us to be alone and talk. Luckily, this practice remained the same. But was he the same person I knew from the first life? If so, should I confide in him about being from the future? Staring at my empty bowl, I said, "Yeah, I'm ready."

Farrell got up, and I did too. Glancing at Dominique, I spotted alarm in her eyes. I set my bowl down on the ground and leaned down to her. Putting my hand behind her head, I pressed my cheek against hers and whispered in her ear. "Infiniti says Trent is fine." I let my words sink in for a second. Then, knowing we needed to act like we normally did, I kissed her lips softly. "I'll be right back," I said casually, yet loud enough for the others to hear and think everything between us was business as usual.

Scooping up my bowl, I followed Farrell to the back of the cabins. We placed our dirty dishes in a large water-filled trough, and then went to the horses. Here alone in the dark, with only sprinkles of light from the stars and a half-moon overhead, I found the cool air crisp and clean inside my lungs. I had forgotten how refreshing it felt to take in such pure air. Drawing in a deep breath, I scanned the area. Five horses grazed nearby—three black and two brown. In the original first life, we let our steeds have free reign around the compound during the day, but at night we kept them tied for safekeeping. Unsure if we did things the same in this new reality, I waited for Farrell to move first.

"Do you want to tell me what that was about?" Farrell asked, patting the side of the nearest horse and leading it to the wooden hitching post.

Approaching the next closest horse, I copied Farrell's actions. Rubbing the side of the horse, I led it to the wooden post, untied one of the ropes already there, and draped it around the horse's neck. "What do you mean?"

"Have you gone mad?" Farrell asked, approaching another horse and leading it to where I stood. "Who is that stranger and why did you bring up Tavion?"

Standing in the night with a brother I didn't know anymore, my thoughts raced. I shrugged my shoulders, trying to act normal. "I don't know why I brought up Tavion. As for Trent, I already told you. He's a friend I met in town."

"He is no friend, Brother. He's a Transhuman and should have announced his affiliation to you. Since he didn't, then it must follow that he is deceiving you and us."

Rubbing the horse between the eyes, I tried to think of something to say that would help Trent. "If he is a Transhuman, then he is unaware. You know as well as I do that Transhumans who let their powers go dormant lose their abilities. Perhaps he is an offspring of such a couple."

"A powerful couple then," Farrell added. "I sensed a lot of innate strength in him. The fact you didn't tells me something is amiss. His force is thick."

"You may be right. Maybe I missed that."

"I certainly hope you are not going soft. We can't afford it, especially with Tavion dead and the new mission upon us."

"I'm not going soft, I can assure you," I said, wondering how I could get intel on the new mission without sounding like I didn't know anything. I approached another horse and directed it to the post.

Picking up a rope, I said, "Any new developments on the mission?"

"None," Farrell said. "Everything is the same."

With the horses in their place and properly tethered, I shoved my hands in my pockets. "Good," I said, trying to sound like I knew what we were talking about. I wondered if I should risk asking about Jake, but decided against it. We had just arrived, so maybe he'd show up later. Or maybe he was dead, too.

Farrell crossed his arms and let out a sigh, as if he'd had the hardest day. "Is everything okay with you and Dominique? I sensed a strangeness between you."

My hairs stood on edge. He sensed something off between us? That wasn't good. "We're fine."

"Would you tell me otherwise?" Farrell prodded.

"Of course," I replied, thinking I needed to figure out what the hell was going on before everything exploded in my face.

Appearing satisfied with my answers, Farrell relaxed his shoulders. He came up to me and clasped me on the arm. "I am glad you are well, Brother."

"Me too, Brother." Putting my hand on his arm in turn, I remembered our bond. Standing close to my brother again after lifetimes of being ripped apart, I mourned the loss of our friendship. A well-spring of sadness released from deep inside me at how he thought I had really turned against him and the others, and how he had fallen in love with Dominique several times over. A lump formed in my throat and I forced it down. "I'd never betray you, Farrell," I said in a half-whisper. "Never."

"Nor I you," he said, eyeing me with a sincerity I had long forgotten. "Are you sure all is well with you?"

"Yes, I'm sure," I said, releasing his arm and pulling myself together. I thought of confiding in him, but didn't. Too much in this time was different, and I needed more answers before I could figure out how to proceed. "Let's get back to the others."

Walking back to the cabins, I saw Stone alone by the dying embers of the fire. Farrell and I joined him. Lit candles adorned the windows of the cabin Dominique shared with her parents. "Dominique has turned in for the night?" I asked.

"Yes, she and Caris both," Stone answered.

"So what do we do tomorrow about the Texan?" Farrell asked.

"We kill him," Stone said matter-of-factly. "Early in the morning before the ladies arise." He kicked at the dirt, finishing off the glowing ash.

"Whoa, wait a second. We kill him? Just like that?" I asked. "You said we would test him."

"I said that for the benefit of my daughter who, for some reason, has found the need to champion the traveler. We will say he escaped in the middle of the night. She does not need to know of our dirty work." Stone narrowed his eyes at me. "We take care of our own. At all cost. And he is not one of us." Stone paused while he kept drilling me with his gaze. "Whatever is the matter with you, Fleet?"

Keeping my hands deep in my pockets, I said, "I know we take care of our own, but can we at least hear him out? Release him back to his people if we find he's no threat? He's been nothing but a friend to me."

Farrell came to my aid. "Fleet has a point, Stone. Perhaps he is aligned with us. Should we not investigate?"

Stone rubbed his face. "Fine. We will interrogate the Texan tomorrow. His answers will determine his fate."

My mind whirled at how different Stone was in this reality. Normally kind and peaceful, this new Stone was the opposite—cold, calculated, and ready to kill. My instincts told me he'd off Trent no matter what the questioning revealed. I couldn't let that happen. I'd have to steal away in the middle of the night, warn Trent, and set him free before the others awoke. After that? I had no idea, but I had to trust I'd come up with something. Realizing I hadn't seen Tiny in a while, I gave the area a quick scan, but found no trace of her. I knew she'd come back and this time I was counting on it. Right now she was the only eyes and ears I had, and I needed an edge on whatever the hell was going on in this life.

~DOMINIQUE~

THE INSIDE OF THE CABIN I SHARED WITH MY MOM AND dad was as cozy and quaint as the outside. Constructed of thick logs, it had that same warm feeling as Richard and Sue's much larger log cabin from my time. My thoughts turned to Richard and Sue, and even Colleen and Jake. Where were they? I dared not ask.

"Tea?" Mom asked.

"Yes, thanks." I took a seat at the small wooden table and studied the room while she heated up a pot of water.

An oversized black iron stove filled one side of the room. Next to that were shelves filled with assorted kitchenware and wash basins. On the other side of the room was a wall with a closed door. My parents' room must've been on the other side. To the far right was a wooden ladder that led to a lofted area. That had to have been where I slept.

Finished with her task, she joined me with two floral patterned teacups. I took a sip of the warm lemon infused tea. The liquid glided down my throat and warmed my insides. "This is really good. Thank you."

"I'm glad you like it." She took a sip of her tea while her eyes glued on me. "So, are you going to tell me what's going on?"

A distant memory sprang to mind. I was sitting at a kitchen table with my old neighbor, Jan. We were sipping tea in her Houston home. At the time, I didn't know if I could trust her, but I eventually told her everything about being hunted. She ended up dying because of me. But how? How did she die? The details of what had happened to her escaped me, though I knew if I thought hard enough I'd remember.

"Dominique," Mom prompted. "What is going on?"

"Going on?" I asked, suddenly pulled back to my reality. "What do you mean?" Everything inside my heart said to trust her, that she was my mom, that I loved her, that she loved me, but my head overrode my emotions. This was an alternate reality, and even though I wanted nothing more than to hug her and tell her everything, nothing felt right.

"I know you as well as I know the sunshine that wakes me every morning." She leaned forward. "Something is off."

Forcing myself to laugh, I said, "I'm tired. That's all."

She tilted her head a little to the right, and furrowed her brow. "Then what is on your right hand?"

Bringing my attention to my hand, I saw a silver

band with connected hearts. I stared at the ring. The glow from the oil lamp on the kitchen table danced around the band, giving it a dreamlike quality. I vaguely recognized the piece of jewelry, yet couldn't remember who had given it to me. I kept my panic deep inside, wondering why I couldn't recall any details about the ring. "Oh, this?" I stalled while I came up with a story. If she had never seen the ring before, then I must've carried it with me through the time jump. "Fleet gave it to me today."

"He did? Today?"

"Yes, he did." I rose to my feet, desperate to end the conversation and escape my mom's probing stare. Looking around the small home, I searched for a bathroom I could duck into, then remembered how during this time most people used outhouses. I faked a yawn and stretched my arms. "You know, I'm exhausted. I'm going to use the outhouse before turning in for the night."

A row of hooks lined the wall by the front door. Two long white shawls and a brown coat hung from the pegs. I grabbed the shawl closest to the door. "I'll be back," I said. Draping the knitted fabric over my shoulders, I exited the cabin as quickly as I could. This was not going well at all. Spying Fleet at the fire with Dad and Farrell, I wondered how things were going with him.

Staring at the group, a tug of homesickness pulled at me. Suddenly my mind filled with Trent. "He gave me the ring," I said out loud to myself. He had been attacked and hauled off. An urgent need to find him blasted through me.

About to head out for him, the sound of a door

swinging behind me stopped me in my tracks. "Dominique," Mom said. "You forgot this." She handed me the oil lamp from the kitchen table.

"Oh, yeah," I said with a laugh. "Thanks."

Wrapping my cold fingers around the metal handle, I started trudging my way to the back of the cabins in the direction where Fleet and Farrell had taken Trent. Finally alone, I studied my surroundings. The horses were tethered to the right. Beyond that, I made out a small rectangular structure and not far from that a small hut. The building had to be the outhouse, the hut had to be where Trent was.

Picking up my pace, I discovered I actually needed to go to the bathroom. Finding the outhouse surprisingly clean and smelling oddly like a Christmas candle, I did my business and then hurried over to where Trent was being held. Stopping at the door, praying he was inside, I cracked the door open a bit, then swung it ajar. My eyes made out the glow of the sizzling ropes. I lifted my lamp to see better, and a body came into view.

"Dominique!" Trent said. He sat on a cot, propped up by the wall.

Closing the door behind me, I rushed to his side. "Oh my God, Trent." Tears spilled onto my cheeks.

"Oh, no, Dominique," he said. "Don't. I'm okay, really."

Setting the lamp on the ground, I timidly touched his face, afraid I'd get zapped, but not caring. A vibration connected at my fingertips as I stroked his cheek. "Trent," I managed to get out between my crying, the pain crushing my heart like a bulldozer. "We should've never come here."

"Shhh," he said, nudging his face under my hand so he could kiss it. "Don't say that, please. We are saving people by being here, including our future child. This will all be over when Fleet kills Tavion."

My tears had started to stop, but picked up again, strangling the words I wanted to get out.

"What?" Trent asked. "What is it?"

Forcing myself to calm enough to clear my throat, I said, "Tavion is already dead."

A look of horror covered Trent's face. "He's dead?"

"Yes," I said, fighting my sobs. "He is. And the others know something is up with us. I can tell. My mom even said something was off." Hearing my voice had risen a few octaves, I forced myself to hush, when an idea sprang to mind. "We need to get out of here. We need to go back home."

Trent closed his eyes. His beautiful face twisted with regret. "We can't," he whispered. "We're here, and we need to finish what we set out to do."

My lip quivered as I considered his words. "B-b-but Tavion is dead. E-e-everything is different."

He looked at me with renewed determination. "Someone else must be the marker if Tavion is dead." His words forced their way through my head. He was right. We couldn't abandon our mission. "Listen," he went on. "You and Fleet need to get me out of here as soon as you can. Together we'll figure out what to do. Besides, with those cops busting into *Abuela's* house, we can't go back even if we wanted to."

"Cops?" I asked, my brain fuzzy and confused.

"Yeah," he said. "The cops. You know, they

stormed into *Abuela's* house right before we time jumped."

I pressed my hand to my lips, wracking my brain for any memory of cops busting into Trent's grandmother's house. In fact, I concentrated hard on the details of our time-jump, but could only remember swirling vapors. My body trembled with fear. "I'm losing it," I confessed to Trent.

"No, you are not." His tone prodded me to snap out of it. "It's stress, Dominique, that's all." His expression gave away his fear that he thought it much more than stress. "You and Fleet need to get away from the others and come back as soon as you can. Can you do that?"

"Yes," I said, renewed with purpose. "I can do that."

Leaning cautiously to avoid the electrified strands, I lighted my lips on his. "I love you."

"I love you, too. Now go. And hurry."

Back outside, I leaned against the wooden door to Trent's prison and set the lamp down. Pulling up my skirt, I used it to wipe my face. *Get Fleet. Free Trent.* Smoothing out my dress, I let out a long breath of air. Repeating the objective over and over in my head, the mantra became a source of hope. All I needed to do now was find Fleet and get him alone.

~FLEET~

Standing around the dying fire with Stone and Farrell, I saw Dominique leave her cabin. Holding an oil lamp to light her way, she moved around to the back of the homes where the horses were. I waited a bit, then excused myself so I could follow her. I figured she'd gone looking for Trent.

The horses let out a friendly snort as I passed by, their bursts of breath visible in the cool air. Pausing mid-step, their huffs reminded me of a different animal. I rubbed the back of my neck, the memory of a dog hovering in the fringes of my mind.

"Did we have a dog?" I asked myself out loud.

"Uh, you did," a ghostly whisper answered.

Spinning around to the source of the sound, I saw Tiny shimmer into view. "You're right," I said to her, memories of Buddy flooding my mind. "His name was…" I struggled to remember every detail of him—black, fluffy, with a long tail that twisted to the side. He used to follow me everywhere. He even slept on my bed with me, curled up in a ball at my feet. What had happened to him? And what did I call him?

"Buddy," she said. "His name was Buddy. He was really cute." She moved closer to me and tilted her head to the side. "Are you okay?"

Dismissing my forgetfulness, I turned my attention to her absence. "Where the hell have you been?"

"Checking out the area," she said. "Sheesh, why?"

"Everything has gone to hell."

"What? How?"

"Stone and Caris are way different. Especially Stone. He wants to kill Trent tomorrow unless we can set him free tonight and get him out of here."

She tried to slam her hands over her mouth, but they moved through her with ease. "Oh, no," she mumbled. "Kill him?"

"That's not even the worst part," I said.

"OMG, there's something worse?"

I lowered my voice and moved closer to her. "Tavion is already dead."

Her big eyes grew even bigger. Her arms dropped to her sides. Her entire translucent form faded like a light switch being dimmed. "No. Way."

Beyond her I caught sight of a light. It had to be Dominique. "Listen Tiny, right now you're our only hope."

"Holy shit," she whispered. "I'm your Obi-Wan."

"Find out what happened to Tavion. Needs to be done quick. Like yesterday."

"Yeah," she said. "I'm on it."

She faded out of view, and I continued on toward the light source and Dominique. The glowing lamp sat on the floor and lit up the area around her legs.

She had lifted her outer skirt and was wiping her face. *Damn*, I thought, recognizing the look of utter despair on her face and knowing she'd been crying. Slowing my approach so I could give her a few seconds, and not wanting to scare her, I said softly, "Hey, Dominique. It's me, Fleet."

She rushed over to me and took my arms in a desperate hold. "I told Trent we have to go back, but he doesn't want to. He says we need to finish what we started, but I don't know." Her tone was pleading and desperate and confused. Fresh tears sprang to her eyes. "He wants us to free him so we can figure out what to do, but I think we need to leave." Her nails dug into my skin as she held on for dear life. "I'm so confused," she confessed. Something in her tone told me she was talking about much more than whether we should stay here or go back to our proper time.

Glancing over my shoulder at the cabins, everything looked so peaceful, but looks were deceiving. Too much was different here. With Tavion dead and so many unknowns, I could see her point, but Trent was right. We couldn't abandon our mission. Plus, another time jump might makes things worse. If Tavion was dead, someone else had taken his place. That person was our new target. We just needed to figure out who it was. "Let's get Trent out of that holding chamber before we do anything else."

A blast of white light shot up into the sky. It soared for a few seconds, then tumbled back down and faded from view. It reminded me of a signal flare for help.

"That can't be good," Dominique whispered.

"No, it can't."

"Fleet!" Farrell shouted from the cabins. His voice

echoed around us. "Dominique! Come back! They're coming!"

Dominique and I stared at each other, both of us unsure about what we should do. "What do you think?" I asked, knowing I wanted to stay and help but letting her make the call. Things were weird, but it didn't feel right to abandon Farrell, especially when I had just told him how I'd never betray him.

She eyed the cabins. "They're still my parents."

"Yeah, they are. And Farrell is still my brother."

"Wait here," she said. With her lamp held high, she let go of my hand and rushed over to Trent's hut. She opened the door, said something, and then came back to me. "We help my parents and the others. But as soon as we can, we come back here for Trent."

"Sounds good to me."

Hurrying back to the others, we were met by Farrell. "Fleet, Dominique," he said with relief. "I was about to go looking for you all." He took Dominique's hand. "Come on," he said to her. "Let's go." Then he said to me, "Hurry on, Fleet. They need you."

I started to lodge an objection, but changed my mind. Whatever was happening seemed to have happened before, and apparently Farrell's role was to usher Dominique away while I stayed to help. Should I go along with the apparent norm of the time? Changing my usual actions would tip him off, and then we might never be able to help Trent.

"Go," Dominique urged me. "Once we get through this we can get back to what we were doing."

"I need to get her out of here," Farrell pressed. "Now."

Whatever was going on, Dominique was still at

risk. Focusing on her and ignoring everything else, I said, "I'll come back for you." I cupped her face and kissed her on the lips without hesitation. This time, she returned the affection. Her lips softened against mine. Her mouth parted with true meaning. It was as if she remembered our deep love in this life. We separated from each other slowly. Our eyes locked in a shared memory of our old selves.

"Be safe," she said.

"You too."

Farrell pulled her further into the woods. Staring at them as they faded from view, I scratched my head. Something was happening that I didn't understand, and as much as I wanted to analyze it, I couldn't. Our home was in danger.

Sprinting into action, I burst into the bustling camp. Caris caught sight of me right away. She was blasting a spark of energy at a pile of fresh logs, creating a new bonfire. "Is Dominique safe?"

"Yes, Farrell has her."

"Good," she said, completing her task. "Now go help Stone with the torches. They'll be here soon."

Torches? We didn't have torches that I recalled, so this was another new thing in this time.

"Hurry, Fleet," she commanded.

Spinning around looking for Stone, I saw him at the far end of the compound. He held a long wooden staff with a ball of fiery energy at the top. He held it out and touched the top of metal pole. When the rods made contact, a buzzing flame ignited atop the post. I dashed over to him.

"Get your staff, Fleet!"

Shit, I was doing everything wrong.

"In the cabin!" Stone yelled.

Zipping into the cabin, I saw an identical staff leaning against the wall. Snatching it up, I shot back out of the structure and set the top aflame with a flick of my wrist. Scanning the area where Stone was, I spied a row of metal poles that lined the compound. We didn't have those in the original first life.

Dashing to the other side of the bonfire, I started lighting the poles like Stone. One by one, they lit up with a touch of my energy flame until a ring of energy fire encircled the compound. Returning to the middle with Stone, we joined Caris. I snuffed out my torch and leaned it against a nearby bench. Save for the sizzling we had created with our circle of flames, and the crackling of the bonfire in the middle, the night filled with an eerie stillness.

"We hear them out," Stone directed. "If they make any sudden movements or threaten us in any way, we blast them." Caris nodded, and then Stone eyed me in turn. "Understood?"

"Yes," I said, thinking if the Tainted were coming, then we could end them here and now. That would fulfill our mission. All I needed to do was provoke them, and then Stone, Caris, and I could blast them to hell. With that done, I could slip away with Dominique, get Trent, and return to our proper time. For once I felt like things were going our way. Finally.

"Why not end this now?" I asked, wanting to prime them for action. "Kill them all while they least expect it?"

"They took one of ours, and we proposed taking one of theirs," Stone said. "Let us see what they say."

My mind spun. They took one of ours? Someone

on our side had been murdered by the Tainted already? Was it Jake? "We should strike," I urged. "Slaughter them before they take anyone else."

Stone circled the area, rubbing his chin, considering my proposal.

"No!" Infiniti yelled, flickering into view. "Fleet, they're—"

The thud of galloping reverberated through the woods. The din grew closer until a group appeared. They reigned in their horses outside the lighted circle and dismounted.

I studied them one by one—Colleen, Richard, Sue and a guy my age I didn't recognize. Colleen had been part of Tavion's group, but had been killed by Farrell when Farrell had turned against Dominique. Richard and Sue were with us, the Pures, and had made a stand against the Tainted in their cabin before meeting their demise. But now they were part of the Tainted? I couldn't believe it. Not them. Richard and Sue were the most loving couple I'd ever known. Even Dominique adored them and referred to them as Uncle Richard and Aunt Sue. As for the guy with them, he bore a strong resemblance to Richard. He had to be Richard and Sue's son. They didn't have children in my first life, but it appeared they did in this reality.

My attention then went back to Infiniti, but she had disappeared. I wondered what she was about to say.

"May I enter the ring?" Colleen asked. Wearing a long green dress, same as Sue, she spoke with authority, so must've been the new leader of the Tainted now that Tavion was dead. I rubbed my fingers together, ready to blast her and the others into smithereens.

"Yes," Stone said. "You may enter."

She crossed into our area with a sizzle, and I realized the circle of torches had activated some sort of energy field around us. *Clever.* Tall and thin with long dark hair and straight bangs, she eyed us each in turn. "We are here to discuss your proposal."

Stone clasped his hands behind his back. "Let me restate the terms, then, so as to avoid any misunderstanding. In exchange for the murder of Tavion, we demand the life of one of yours."

Whoa, what? Tavion was with us? He was a Pure? He was murdered by the Tainted? My gut tightened. Every hair on my body stood on edge. I tried to hide my shock, but Colleen must've noticed. She zeroed in on me, her laser-like stare penetrating me like a probe. I held my ground and returned her glare, determined to hide my surprise. I even cleared my mind, in case she had the ability to read my thoughts.

"We agree to give you a life, but it shall be done on *our* terms," Colleen said, her attention settling back on Stone. "We will allow you to place your death mark on one of our own, on the condition that this chosen one will have nine lifetimes to remove the mark. Nine chances to escape death."

Colleen's words seem to float in the air, as if fighting their way into my comprehension. We were going to mark one of *them*? But Dominique wasn't with them, she was with us. Nothing was making sense.

"Nine chances to be killed," Stone repeated. "You

will do that? Exact that type of sentence? Death nine times over?"

Colleen let out a sigh. "Yes, if it means you will honor the code and stop interfering with humankind, then we are willing to take the risk of death nine times."

"The code? Damn, the code! They are murderers, Colleen," Stone spat out. "These humans that you defend. Look at the wars they have caused! The American Revolution, the War of 1812, the Mexican War, the Civil War. And now, they are killing the first inhabitants of this land! All they do is kill. It is all they know, and it will not stop. I can promise you that. Greed. Power. Revenge. Hate. These are their greatest traits."

"It is not for us to say what they will or will not do," Colleen responded, keeping calm. "As for their traits, they offer so much more—love, kindness, generosity."

Stone formed a fist. "Those traits are inferior to them!"

Colleen moved closer to Stone. "As they are inferior to you?" Her face took on an expression of sadness. "You were not always so."

"Humans will destroy this world, and take us along with it," Stone replied, pleading with Colleen to see his point of view. "Don't you see that?"

"Then they destroy the world," Colleen said. "And us along with it."

Slowly, I began to realize the horror of this life. A sick feeling spread in my gut, wrestling it tight. Despair filled every inch of my body.

Colleen and her people were the Pures.

We were the Tainted.

"We ask to choose the one to be marked," Colleen said, going back to the terms. "Is that acceptable?"

"That is acceptable," Stone said. He shot a smoky blast at the ground in front of her boots. "Now go," he ordered, his hand raised and ready to level another blast at her. "Before I lose my patience with you."

Colleen appeared unfazed by the threatening move. "We will return with our chosen one three days hence."

Colleen left us. Her party mounted their rides. Watching them trot away, my brain scrambled to process everything I had learned culminating in the horrifying realization that we were the bad guys. We were the ones responsible for murder and destruction. We were the ones filled with hate and revenge. We were the ones who'd hunt down an innocent life nine times over. We were nothing but pure evil.

~DOMINIQUE~

As I was pulled into the woods by Farrell, my mind labored to figure out what was happening to me. I had kissed Fleet, *really* kissed him. Sparks of remembering his touch and what it felt like to be with him blossomed not only in my heart, but in my thoughts. When we dashed past the small log cabin where Trent was being held, a surge of guilt came over me. I couldn't have feelings for Fleet, I couldn't. I was in love with Trent. He was the one for me. No one else. *Right?*

Stumbling over a log in my path, I almost fell face first, but managed to stay upright. My tangled thoughts had tripped me up, and I was pissed. I refused to take on the role of damsel in distress. Angry at not knowing what was happening, I jerked my hand away from Farrell's grasp. "I got it," I spat at him, not wanting to be dragged around anymore. "Now back off."

He slowed down, gave me a puzzled look, and then picked up his pace again. "As you wish."

"That's right," I muttered back to him.

We skirted around a cluster of tall thin trees, then stopped in front of a mound of thick brush. Suddenly, I knew exactly where I was. Handing Farrell the lamp I had managed to hold onto, I pulled away at the shrubs and exposed a wooden door.

"This door leads to a cellar," I said, in surprised recognition. "We hide here sometimes." My words sounded like they didn't belong to me, as if someone faraway had spoken on my behalf. How did I know this underground room was here? I had no recollection of any of my past lives. Were my memories filtering through now that I was inhabiting this time and space?

"I know," Farrell responded. He was confused at my behavior, I could tell, and how could I blame him? I was baffled too. "Come on," he beckoned. "They are near."

The stairs creaked with each step down. The room reeked of dirt and mud. My ears muffled the further down we got. Shelves lined the cramped room at the bottom. A table and four chairs took up most of the space. I placed the oil lamp on the table, and sat down. I drew the shawl tight around my shoulders.

Torches adorned the corners of the room. With a flick of his wrist, Farrell lit them with his energy stream. The four flames warmed the place quickly and provided more light. With the room fully lit, I noticed a dark feather resting on the ground by my foot. I let out a gasp.

"What is it?" Farrell asked.

Scooping up the plume, I held it out to him. Farrell studied the object. His golden hued hair almost sparkled by the firelight. His perfectly angular features should've awakened something inside me for him, but they didn't. Even though we had fallen in love several lifetimes over, I had no feelings for him. Instead, a growing affection for Fleet had started to take over. It was strong and powerful. It was even making me forget my love for… I searched my brain for a name but couldn't find it.

What is happening to me?

Examining the feather, I asked Farrell, "Does this feather mean anything to you?"

Farrell gave it a curious look. He took it and eyed it closely. "No, it does not." He gently placed it back in my hand. "Does it mean something to you?"

I set it on the table with care, as if it were a foreign object I shouldn't be handling. "Well, not this one here, but yes, a feather, a white one, represents…" I cut my sentence short. Farrell had given me a feather to help me remember him when my memories over the lifetimes had started to fade. Scraping my chair against the dirt floor, I stood upright with a jolt. "Oh my God. I know what's happening."

Farrell's eyes narrowed a bit. "And what is that?"

"I'm forgetting everything, and this life is taking over," I whispered to myself, terrified of losing myself and becoming someone I didn't know. Everything I had been through, all the people I loved, those I had lost, every single thing I knew, was fading away.

The person I love. What is his name?

"You are what?" Farrell asked, unable to hear my words since I had spoken them so faintly. He came closer. He lighted his hand on my shoulder. "Dominique, you are not yourself."

"Not at all," I said, sinking back down to my seat.

Showers of goose bumps lined my skin. Even though the room had warmed significantly, a different kind of chill settled in my bones. I drew my shawl in even tighter, my mind on overdrive. If I was forgetting who I was and merging with myself from this time, when would I forget everything? How long did I have still being me? And was the same thing happening to Fleet?

I buried my face in my hands and starting mumbling things about my life, testing my recall. "My name is Dominique Wells. My parents are Stone and Caris. We are Transhumans, part of the Pures. Tavion, marked me. My parents shielded me to protect me, yet Tavion found me and killed me over and over again. I don't remember any of my past lives. I only know my current life, life nine. In this life, I defeated Tavion with the help of…." My voice trailed off. Who had helped me? I couldn't remember.

"What are you saying?" Farrell asked, standing with a ball of light in his hand aimed at me. Seeing him like that unlocked a deluge of memories of him protecting me, holding me, kissing me, dying for me.

"You," I said. "You were my main protector."

Fire from the torches created dancing shadows across the earthen walls. Ignoring the ball of vapor-izing energy in Farrell's hand, I thought of my memo-ries. I was forgetting the most current stuff first. It was as if my mind was a computer, and my most recent files were being deleted before the older ones. Eying my once protector and someone I had loved over several lifetimes, I asked, "Can I trust you?'

Farrell powered down his energy blast. He

lowered his hand. Concern and empathy spread across his face. "Of course you can, Dominique. You know that."

Trent! His name is Trent!

Relieved at remembering Trent's name, I blew out a breath, when something else occurred to me. Trent didn't exist during this time, so his memories would stay his own and not be taken over. A glimmer of hope set in, along with a sense of shame at having forgotten his name.

"What," Farrell urged. "What is it?"

I was about to tell him how Fleet, Trent, and I were from the future, when a wooden door to our underground hideaway creaked open.

"Dominique?"

"Fleet!" I called, jumping to my feet with relief.

His heavy boots thudded down the stairs. He threw Farrell a cautious look. He took my hand. "Come on. The threat is over."

Whatever he had experienced was bad. And by the urgency in his voice, was not over.

"What happened?" Farrell asked.

"Stone can fill you in. I need to be with Dominique right now."

Farrell rubbed his face. "Hold on, Brother. There is something afoot with you two, as well as your friend from Texas. I demand to know what it is."

Antsy and on edge, Fleet's leg bounced with nervous energy. "Farrell. Brother. I swear to you, I will fill you in on everything, but not right now. There is business I must attend to with Dominique first. Please, understand."

Farrell gave a long pause, then said, "I do not understand, but I will honor your wishes."

"Thank you," Fleet said. "And one more thing. Don't mention any of this to the others. Can you do that?"

Farrell gave a slow nod. "I will not mention this to the others, unless a situation arises requiring me to do so."

"Fair enough," Fleet said.

Taking the lamp, I followed Fleet out of the underground room. We tracked through the woods at a fierce pace, as if running for our lives. Once we got far enough away, we stopped. Bending over and catching my breath, I waited for my breathing to normalize before I spoke.

"What happened?" I panted, wondering what could've been so bad that Fleet needed to retreat to an isolated place to talk.

He ran his fingers through his dark hair. "We are so fucked."

"You have no idea," I added, wondering if what he had to say to me was the same thing I had to say to him. "You go first. Then I'll tell you what I figured out."

He paced around with his hands balled into fists, ready to punch someone. "We are the Tainted."

My breathing hitched. My heart stopped beating. An icy chill raced down my spine. "What?" My brain sorted his words, having a hard time believing what he had said. "We are...what?"

"You, me, Farrell, Stone, Caris. We are the bad guys. Tavion was part of our group, but he was killed by the Pures. And Jake, I don't even think he exists in this timeline we created."

Suddenly, I thought of how the Pures had green eyes and the Tainted had dark eyes. I shone the light at Fleet's face. I gasped. "Your eyes, they're dark." I brought the lamp to my face. "What color are mine?"

Fleet peered at me. "They're dark."

"We have dark eyes. Why didn't we notice that before?" My hands shook something fierce. I carefully set the lamp down before it could tumble out of my grasp and set fire to the whole area. I sank to my knees. "This can't be."

"Colleen is the leader of the Pures," Fleet said, expanding on what he had learned. "Richard and Sue are with Colleen, along with a guy I think is Richard and Sue's son." Fleet knelt down before me. "Stone proposed to mark one of the Pures as punishment for what was done to Tavion. Colleen agreed, but asked to pick the person and asked for nine lifetimes to remove the mark."

My hand moved to the back of my neck. I wasn't marked because I was one of the bad guys? Then why was I being protected and dragged to the underground room by Farrell? And what poor soul would end up carrying the burden of having to live multiple lives with a death target?

"What about you. What did you learn?" Fleet asked me.

What he had said was way worse than anything I could've imagined, but he had to know what I had figured out because it was bad, too. "We are losing our memories. At least I am. I suspect you are, too."

Fleet scanned the area as he considered my words.

"I forgot the name of my dog earlier. And I feel like my recall is fuzzy."

"I think our identities from this time are slowly taking over our minds." I almost told him how I was having genuine feelings for him, when the glint of a ring on my finger distracted me. I held up my hand. "I have a ring?" I asked, wondering how I had acquired it. "I, uh, it, umm…." I slammed my palm against my forehead. "Who gave this to me?"

Fleet took my hand and touched the silver band with two connecting hearts. "This came from…" His words trailed off. "It's on the tip of my tongue," he murmured. "…Trent! I remember you telling me Trent gave it to you."

A renewed sense of hope sprang in me as I remembered Trent and our love. "Yes. Trent. He's my boyfriend. I love him. We have to free him and…" I couldn't finish my thought because the percolating notion in my brain had vanished.

Fleet helped me to my feet. "Let's get to him right the hell now before this whole cursed life comes crashing down on us. He's not from this time, so he should remember what's going on."

I bent to pick up the oil lamp, but Fleet said, "Forget that damn thing." He lit up a ball of light in his palm and held his arm out. "Come on."

Making our way in the cold air through the brush and trees, apprehension mounted inside of me. Images of past memories started popping up in my brain—Tavion's skeletal face as he killed me in the red desert. Trent bringing me back to life when he touched the cross around my neck his grandmother had given me. Farrell's protective arms around me.

Fleet getting in my face and calling me a traitor. So many images raced through my head, but they were getting jumbled and mixed up.

Forcing myself not to freak out, I concentrated on my breathing. Inhaling the crisp, cool air for a count of four, I held it for seven seconds, then let it trickle out of my mouth nice and slow. Someone had taught me that technique, but I couldn't remember who. Pushing that aside, I forced myself to think of Trent. I repeated his name over and over in my head, my sanity clinging to him with everything I had.

The small hut where Trent was being held came into view. A bit of relief started edging out my panic. Everything appeared still and quiet, which was a good sign. Fleet must've echoed my feelings, because he glanced at me from over his shoulder and gave me a confident nod. I nodded back. *This is happening*, I said to myself. *Everything is going to work out.*

~ T R E N T ~

DARKNESS SUFFOCATED THE STRUCTURE I FOUND MYSELF in when I regained consciousness after being attacked. Tugging and pulling against the sizzling energy rope that bound me tight only made the pain worse, so I sat and waited, trying to be as motionless and calm as possible until Dominique returned. She said something was happening and that she and Fleet were going to investigate. Worry for her strangled me. Her bloodshot eyes and fearful appearance played over and over in my mind. I told myself she'd be okay, that everything would work out, but I had a hard time believing myself.

Alone and immersed in doubt, I thought of how stupid we were for believing we could come to first life without consequences. What were we thinking? The last time I had time traveled, I ended up getting shot by a crazy nun and left in the past. Luckily, I had managed to make it back to my proper time in one piece. Back then, an ambulance driver and his son had helped me. Even Abigail, the young Transhuman girl who was part of the Pures, had come to me in ghost form and offered aid. I perked up with renewed hope. I was a Transhuman, a Supreme with immense abilities. I didn't know how to control what I could do, and sometimes summoning my powers ended up yielding disastrous results, but maybe I could tap into my potential and ask someone for help. I refused to sit around and do nothing.

Edging up against the wall, I planted my feet firmly on the ground. I closed my eyes and cleared my mind. "This is Trent Avila," I said out loud. "I need help." I waited a few seconds. I slit my eyes open. Nothing.

Letting out an exasperated grunt, I closed my eyes and tried again. This time, I envisioned my blue aura, the depths of the colors burning clear in my mind. "This is Trent Avila. I need help. Now. Please."

The ground beneath my feet vibrated. A humming filled the small enclosure. The faint din turned to whisperings. Snapping my eyes open, I perked up my ears, trying to decipher the words. Although I couldn't make any out, I could tell the voice was communicating in Spanish.

"I can't hear you. *No te escucho.*" The soft murmuring grew louder and quicker. "*Más despacio, más despacio. Por favor,*" I pleaded, desperate for the voice to slow down so I could make out the messages.

"*No está solo,*" a female voice said.

I'm not alone?

The whisperings shut off. A different vibration invaded the room. The hum pierced deep inside of me. My senses soared to red alert. A green vapor came into view. The smoky plume grew tall and wide until it took on the form of a person. Pressing my back against the wall, suddenly panicked at what I had done, I waited to see who'd appear. Long black hair, tall and thin, she held her blazing green staff at the ready and pointed it at my head.

"Colleen?" I gulped.

Keeping her weapon aimed at my forehead, she gave me a suspicious yet curious look. "You know me? How?"

There was no way I could explain how I knew her, so I settled on half-truths. "I've heard of you. You're part of—"

A charge exploded outside my walls. Dust sprinkled down from the crude ceiling. The structure rocked from side to side. Unfazed by the calamity unfolding outside my prison, Colleen demanded, "Reveal your affiliation, or suffer death."

Surges of electricity blasted outside, as if Armageddon itself rained down on us. I needed to say something before she made good on her promise and blasted me, but what?

"*Dile la verdad*," the voice from earlier whispered at my ear.

"The truth?" I asked the voice out loud, questioning the wisdom of the advice.

Colleen moved her staff closer to me. Almost pressed against my forehead, the glowing tip heated my skin. "Yes, the truth," she demanded, thinking I had asked the question of her.

Flashes of light from outside made their way through the slats of timber. An unknown male voice shouted. Fleet hollered a warning. Desperate to get out of my charged shackles so I could help

Dominique and Fleet, I blurted, "My name is Trent Avila. I'm from the future. I'm one of the good guys. One of the Pures."

Colleen stepped back. She lowered her staff. "A Pure? From the future?"

I wrestled with the sizzling cords, zapping myself in the process, fuming because I didn't know how to channel my aura, and terrified about what was happening beyond my four walls. "Yes! I am!"

She lowered her staff and hollered, "Retreat!" Her voice boomed out like a supersonic alarm. She slammed her shimmery weapon against the ground. A cascade of green detonated. I turned my face away from the heat, expecting death, when my body slipped into a free fall. I crashed onto a grassy surface with a thud.

Lying there, I realized my binds were gone. Scrambling to my feet, my legs weak and wobbly, I found myself surrounded by Colleen, Richard, Sue, and a guy my age with long hair. The foursome held staffs that lit up the area with a bright glow.

"What is this?" I asked, searching for the cabins but only seeing trees and brush. "Where am I? What happened to the others?" And then I did a double-take. Richard and Sue were with Colleen? How? Colleen was Tainted. Richard and Sue were part of the Pures. I started backing away from my new captors.

"This is Trent Avila from the future," Colleen announced, eyeing her group. "He claims to know me." She cast her stare back on me. "Do you know anyone else here?"

I thought of the voice from earlier that encouraged me to tell the truth, and for some reason I trusted the source. Besides, there was no use lying now. "I know Richard and Sue. But they're not part of the Tainted like you. They're with the Pures, or at least they are, or were, in my time."

"He thinks we're Tainted?" the long-haired guy asked.

"Wait a second." I jabbed my finger at Colleen. "I know exactly who the hell you are. All of you. You're the Tainted."

Continuing to edge away from them, I thought of taking off in a sprint, when Richard advanced with caution. "Hey, Trent Avila. You're wrong. We are not the Tainted."

Colleen held up her hands, as if imploring me to believe them. "We are the Pures. The others back there that had you, *they* are the Tainted."

Richard came even closer. "Look at my eyes."

Edging up to him, I saw green. The mark of a Pure. Terror struck me. My thoughts jumbled. If these people were the Pures, then Stone, Caris, and the others were the Tainted? We had time traveled to an alternative reality where alliances were switched? If what they said was true, then Dominique, Fleet, and even Farrell were the bad guys? I couldn't believe it. "No, no, no," I mumbled. "This can't be." I shoved my hands in my jean pockets. "I'm not saying another damn thing until you tell me what the hell's going on."

Colleen's face softened. Her shoulders relaxed. "Come with us, Trent Avila. Let us go to our cabin and we'll explain everything."

"It's just Trent. You don't have to call me by my full name."

"As you wish, Trent." She walked off. Richard and Sue followed. The guy stayed behind, eyeing me as if I were an alien from another planet. With my strange clothes, who could blame him? I doubted they'd ever met a time traveler before. Separated from my friends and in a strange woodsy area with people who claimed to be the good guys, I considered my options. Follow them and figure out what was going on, or strike out on my own and search for Dominique and Fleet.

"If we were Tainted, you'd be dead," he said.

He had a point, but I was still on the fence about what to do. A strong wind swept through the trees, rustling the leaves. My body shivered from the cold.

"My name is Max. Richard and Sue are my parents."

The similarities came into focus. Max looked exactly like Richard—light colored hair, a long thin nose. How did I not see it before? He started after Colleen and the others. "Do what you want," he called over his shoulder. "But if you go back, they will kill you. And if you call again, we're not coming."

They had heard me? That's why Colleen appeared? "Wait!" I hurried to catch up to him. "You guys rescued me?"

"Yes," Max answered. "You're welcome."

"Thanks," I muttered.

Deciding to take my chances with my unlikely saviors, I went with them to their camp. Trudging through the woods, my mind sorted through the events since arriving in this time. Stone, Caris, and Farrell had attacked me. They had thrown me, tethered and immobile, in a makeshift jail. Their actions didn't match those of the Pures. At least, not the ones I knew. Replaying everything in my mind, I began to realize the truth of Colleen's claims. The people we thought were the Pures, were the Tainted. Dominique and Fleet had no way of knowing the state of alliances in this time, but I wondered if they had figured it out. The energy battle outside my hut seemed to suggest so. I prayed they weren't dead and that they were able to keep their cover.

After walking a few miles, we entered an open area with a two-story log cabin. Half the size of the nearly identical cabin in this area from my time, I figured Colleen and the others lived here. I examined the space when we walked in—small kitchen, sitting room, fireplace. A narrow staircase led upstairs, probably to the bedrooms.

"You all have a cabin almost exactly like this in my time. It was Richard and Sue's cabin. But I didn't know them to have any kids."

"Interesting," Richard mumbled. "Well, we have one now."

"Lucky you," Max said with a grin. He flicked his wrist and lit a fire in the fireplace. He sat on the stone hearth, arms crossed, stare still glued on me with a look of wonder mixed with distrust.

"Tell us about your time and why you are here," Sue said.

Colleen leaned her staff in the corner of the room near the fireplace. "Spare no detail. Understanding where you are from will help us figure out your purpose."

My purpose? My job was to help Fleet travel to this time so he could take out Tavion before he could mark Dominique. But now I was here, Dominique, too. Tavion was dead, and alliances were switched. I had no idea what I was supposed to do. I ran my fingers through my hair and took a seat in a wooden chair.

With my elbows on my knees and my hands folded together, I decided to put my trust in them and told them the story of Dominique's final life. How Tavion marked Dominique. How Stone, Caris and Farrell fought to protect her and remove her mark for lifetimes. How Fleet infiltrated the Tainted, and was so good at his job everyone thought he had really turned evil. How Colleen had been Tainted, but had hidden herself among the Pures. How Dominique had eventually killed Tavion, but hadn't changed her fate of being hunted. I explained every last detail, leading up to the fact that I had helped Fleet transport to this time so he could kill Tavion before he could mark Dominique in the first place in order to spare her future child from the same fate. "But Dominique and I transported, too. We weren't supposed to come here."

Sue's mouth fell open. "Fleet and Dominique are also from the future? And Dominique is with child?"

"Yes, they're with me. And no, Dominique is not with child, not yet anyway. That child, our child actually, will suffer the same fate as Dominique."

"You are her betrothed in the future?" Colleen asked.

"Yes."

"And her mark will be passed down." Colleen said in a half-whisper. "Interesting."

Thick silence hovered in the room as everyone processed my words. Clad in their civil war era attire,

I studied their outfits. The men wore dark pants, white long-sleeved shirts, and work boots. The women had on long green dresses. Looking down at my jeans, t-shirt, and tennis shoes, I most certainly didn't belong.

"It cannot be chance," Richard said to Colleen.

Colleen pursed her lips. "Of course it is not chance. There is no such thing."

My heart started beating out of control. My palms grew sweaty. "What can't be chance?"

Colleen circled the room. She stopped in front of the fire. The tongues of flame from behind her made her appear ablaze herself, like a phoenix. She gestured at her companions. "I am the leader of the Pures. Stone and the others are the Tainted. Stone has always been the leader, and we recently killed Tavion."

"I know," I swallowed. "I heard about that." Still trying to grapple with the switched loyalties, I asked, "What about Fleet? Who's he with?"

"Originally a member of the Tainted, we turned him," Colleen explained. "He stays with them to help us gain valuable information."

"He's a spy in this time, too?" I asked.

"Yes," Max chimed in. "And a good one. He did an excellent show of blending with the Tainted tonight. His blasts nearly got me, as did Dominique's."

A ripple of shock coursed through my body. "Dominique's? Are you saying she has power?"

"Yeah," Richard said. "A lot of power. She's a superconductor and the deadliest of us all. She has the ability to take out a region as big as Michigan itself. That's why she's hidden whenever we're around, to make sure she doesn't rage out."

Colleen came close to me. "Are you saying she has no power in your time?"

"None at all." Drawing in a deep breath, I thought of how I had never been able to see Dominique's aura. Now, in this time, she had power, and was using it. I feared what else may have changed in her since arriving here.

Trying to analyze everyone and their connection to each other, my mind drifted back to Colleen's comment about chance. I still had no idea what she had meant. "Colleen, what did you mean about chance?"

"Let me explain by giving you some background information," she began. "Tavion has always been the most ruthless one of the Tainted. We terminated him before he could slaughter a camp of unsuspecting humans."

Horrified, I held up my hand to pause her. "The Tainted are killing camps of people? Why?"

"The Tainted are murderers," Richard seethed. "Killing people because they think humankind unworthy of this planet."

"They believe regular humans will lead to the eventual destruction of all life," Sue added.

"We did not want to eliminate Tavion, it is not our way, but he forced our hand," Colleen continued. "We do not like to use our powers to interfere with humankind, but will do so when required. Which leads me to tonight. Before you called out to us, we met with Stone and Caris and the others at their camp. They had demanded retribution for what we had done to Tavion. A life. One of our own. We gave them our consent, but asked for nine lifetimes to remove the death mark of whoever would bear this burden. We are to choose a marked one to be presented in three days." Her eyes narrowed a bit. "It is no coincidence you all arrived at this moment in time."

"I came to change things, and I still can," I whispered. "Even with all the differences between my time and this one."

"I believe so," Colleen said. "But how?"

I had risen to my feet, not even realizing it. The fire crackled. The wind outside howled against the windows. My mind took off in a million directions. "My mission was to help Fleet get here so he could kill Tavion before he could mark Dominique, but everything has flipped. Dominique is one of the Tainted, Tavion is dead, and their leader is Stone."

"Stone will be the one to perform the marking," Colleen tacked on, making sure I understood his role.

"What am I supposed to do, then? Still kill the marker? Dominique's dad?" My throat tightened with despair. "I can't do that. That would completely screw up the whole space-time-continuum thing, much more than it already is. And I'm pretty sure Dominique won't let Fleet do it either, assuming he'd even want to." I threw my hands up in frustration. "Who will we be saving anyway? If this life continues on course, the mark won't even pass down through Dominique, right?"

"It will still pass down, but through someone else," Colleen said. "If we follow this course, we will still have to present one of our own to be marked.

Understand?" The quiet in the room magnified her voice, making her words almost echo inside of me.

I looked away from the group. Colleen was right. The mission was always about more than Dominique, it was about humankind. Besides, I had the feeling that no matter what happened, Dominique would somehow always be in danger.

Racing through everything I had learned, I came to the quick realization that I needed to stay the course: save the marked one, whoever that might be, that person's future child, and all of humanity in the process, but how? How could I do it without killing Dominique's dad?

"You're right, Colleen," I admitted, turning to face the group. "The mission is much bigger than any one person. It's about all of us, both now and in the future."

"Correct," Colleen agreed. "And you are here, right now, a Pure from the future, altering reality with your presence."

Transplanted in a different time and place, I thought of her word choice—altering. It sparked a memory of something Farrell had taught me about Transhumans. "Energy cannot be created or destroyed. It can only be transformed," I said, quoting Farrell.

"That's right," Richard said.

*Energy can only be transformed. ...Altered...*I repeated those words over and over in my head. Fleet, Dominique, and I were here, and our presence had altered things. What if I could undo that? What if instead of taking out the marker, I could change him?

"Keep working the problem," Colleen said to me a in a low voice.

Focusing on her, I thought of her wisdom until another wise person popped in my mind—my great grandmother Carmen. She had used the ritual known as *limpia* to expel the evil that had taken a hold of Dominique when we had traveled to 1930. What if I used a similar method as Carmen, first tying up the Tainted with the same sort of energy rope they had used to bind me. Once they were immobile, I could send my strength into them and force theirs out. I envisioned a battle of laser beams. The bigger and brighter light would outshine the smaller. Could mine be bigger than theirs? Would that even work?

"You know what to do, don't you," Colleen prodded.

Staring at the fire, I thought of how heat transformed logs into ash. I certainly didn't want to do something like that to the Tainted. I simply wanted their auras, or force, or power, or whatever you wanted to call it, changed. Rubbing my head, I started to explain the ancient ritual. Quiet at first, my voice grew louder with each word. "I'm Mexican-American. My culture is rich with custom and tradition with a strong connection to the supernatural. My ancestors use a ritual known as *limpia* to remove illness, or even evil, from a person. It's done by rubbing an egg over someone. The ceremony transfers whatever negativity is inside of a person into the egg."

"What?" Max asked, muffling a laugh. "You want us to use eggs against the Tainted?"

"No," I said, understanding how absurd I must've sounded to someone who didn't understand my customs. Ignoring his quip, I asked Colleen, "Can you all rope the Tainted with your energy streams and immobilize them? Like the way I was bound when you found me?"

"It can be done," Colleen said.

"And then what?" Richard asked.

"And then," I made hand gestures, as if pushing the air away from me, visualizing an energy-driven *limpia*. "I send my aura into theirs and snuff theirs out."

"You think your energy can transform theirs?" Colleen asked.

I shrugged. "Maybe."

Richard clapped his hands once. "Maybe works for me."

"Me too," Max said.

"Why not," Sue added.

Colleen retrieved her staff. "And that is why you are here, Trent Avila. You will be presented as the marked one. Once close enough, we will initiate your plan. We can work out the details tomorrow. For now, we need rest."

My plan sounded so simple and doable, but after everyone went to sleep, images of how it would go down spun in my head with the end result being the same. We were all probably gonna die.

~DOMINIQUE~

TAKING ONE LAST LOOK AROUND THE AREA, FLEET AND I advanced toward the hut where Trent was being held. Like a burglar approaching its target, I quieted my breathing and softened my steps. Fleet mimicked my carefulness, extinguishing the light in his hand and slowing his stride. We were almost to the structure, when Fleet stopped. He pushed me behind me. "I sense a –"

A vibrating hum filled my ears. A green burst of light exploded from inside the four walls where Trent was. A guy my age with long hair appeared before us. He eyed us with caution. Something familiar about him tugged at my brain. Did I know him in this time?

"We mean no harm here," he announced. "Colleen has a few questions for your visitor. We will leave when she is finished."

Hatred for the guy boiled in my veins. I shoved Fleet out of the way and flung my arm in his direction. Crackles of lightning exploded from my fingertips. The surge felt wild and exhilarating, filling me with energy and exuberance.

The guy dodged my assault. "Stop her!" he called out.

About to lodge another blow, a firm grip on my wrist prevented me from attacking. I spun around to find Fleet with a look of alarm splashed across his face. "Don't," he implored. "He's—"

"—the enemy," I spat out, jerking my arm from his grasp with renewed strength. I shot a stream of strikes at the guy, each one bigger than the last, determined to take him out.

"Stop!" Fleet hollered.

Unable to continue avoiding my attacks, the guy hurled his own volleys at me, though each effort fell short of its mark. Was he avoiding me on purpose? Now at my side, Fleet flung his own series of blasts, but I could tell his strikes were defensive only and not intended for contact.

"What are you doing?" I seethed. "You have better aim than that!"

"He's one of the good guys, Dominique. Remember?" he pleaded. "So are we."

What? My arms fell to my side as my brain searched for the truth. Fleet was right. We were also the good guys, but here in this time we were evil. Tears stung my eyes at the realization of how muddled my thoughts and memories were. I brought up my trembling hands and stared at them, marveling at the power within me, but also petrified at who I was in this life.

Mom, Dad, and Farrell burst onto the scene.

"Attack!" Farrell cried out. They started hurling

their own energy streams at the guy. Part of me wanted to join them, while another part of me didn't want to hurt anyone.

Saved from having to make a choice, a female voice hollered over the fracas, "Retreat!" An explosion of light discharged from Trent's hut. Green hues bathed the area. When the emerald beams faded, the guy was gone.

"Trent," I whispered, rushing to the hut and flinging the door open. The room was empty. Trent was gone. Not a trace of him, or whoever was in here with him, remained.

Fleet came up behind me. "Shit," he whispered.

Our plan of rescuing Trent had been taken away from us. We were screwed.

Dad grabbed Fleet's arm. "Why was she exposed? Why wasn't she hidden?"

Mom separated Dad and Fleet. "Stop it," she commanded. "Dominique is fine. That is all that matters." She glanced my way. "You are fine, right?"

"Yes. I am." I patted my arms and chest to be sure. "No injuries."

"Good," Dad said. He entered the holding room and paced around. "Now, why would Colleen break the treaty and whisk away your friend from Texas?" He raised his brow and side-eyed Fleet.

"The treaty was not broken. Max announced they were here to talk. It was Dominique who threw the first blow. As for the traveler, I have no idea why they took him."

Max. The name became clear in my mind. Memories of him filtered through. He was Richard and Sue's son. We hated each other.

"Good job, Dominique," Farrell said. "Too bad you didn't get him."

"She could have been killed," Dad admonished. "We *all* could have been killed. There is nothing good about that."

"You're right, Stone. My apologies," Farrell offered.

"If they had laid a hand on Dominique, things could have ended much differently." Mom rubbed my arm. "But they didn't, so all is well."

Laid a hand on me? We would've been killed? I had no idea what she was talking about, but it didn't matter. Trent was taken by the Pures.

"So what do we do about them taking our friend?" I asked, worried sick about Trent, but comforted by the fact that he was with the good guys now. He'd be safe with them, I hoped. "He has no role in our quarrel. He is an innocent traveler."

Farrell shrugged her shoulders. "What do we care about him?"

"Agreed, let them do what they will," Dad added. "We have more important matters to attend to now that Colleen must select one of their own to be marked. That is our main focus now."

I gulped. Flashes of my struggle with Tavion entered my mind. The overriding need to prevent that from happening again, to myself, my child, or anyone else, overcame me. "Maybe we should rethink that."

"What?" Farrell asked. "We are due retribution, Dominique."

"I know, but maybe we should forget about…." My voice trailed off when I realized how absurd and out of character I must've sounded to them. I pinched the area between my eyes. "Nevermind."

Mom placed her hand on my forehead. "You really are not yourself, daughter."

"I do feel kind of," I searched for the right word, "unwell."

All eyes were on me. Mom and Dad wore worried expressions. Farrell, on the other hand, watched me with keen mistrust. His gaze bore deep into me, as if searching for a truth he knew I was hiding. He didn't trust me or Fleet, but had promised not to say anything. But for how long? We were losing our memories, and now Trent had been taken. Could we find him before Fleet and I lost ourselves completely? Before Farrell discovered the truth about us?

"Fleet," Mom directed. "You and Dominique stay in the guest cabin tonight so Dominique can recover from whatever is ailing her."

Fleet took my hand. "Of course, Caris. I will see to her."

Relieved to be away from the others, we made our way as casually as possible to the cabin. "Don't look back," Fleet whispered.

"Not a chance," I uttered under my breath.

My hands tingled from the power that had coursed through them. Gripping Fleet's strong hand, as if his touch could somehow ground me, I forced myself to picture something from my time. A peaceful lake sprang to mind. I thought of the gravel jogging trail around it, and the bench where…. What about the bench? I knew that bench was special, but couldn't recall anything specific. *Think of my house*, I instructed myself. The house sat across the street from the lake. Two-story. Red brick. I lived there with my mom and dad, and then Farrell moved in. He was…. Oh no, who was he to me again? Panic gripped my gut. *Stop freaking out,* I ordered myself. *Think of something else and you'll remember.* Focusing on my street, the memory of a friend filtered through. Wild hair. Big, brown eyes. What was her name?

"Here we are," Fleet said, opening the door for me.

We entered the small, peaceful cabin. It looked exactly like the home I shared with my parents— living space and bedroom downstairs, a loft upstairs. Two wooden rocking chairs faced the stone fireplace. I sank into one of the chairs and brought my legs to my chest, hugging them tightly.

"I have power," I said, still marveling at my strength. "I had no idea."

"Back in our original first life, you had power, too, like the rest of us. When your parents started shielding you to protect you after you were marked, your powers went dormant."

Running my hands over the rough fabric of my dress, I thought of the incredible force brimming within me. I longed to experience the sensation again, though I knew I shouldn't. The rush had connected me to the Tainted. Hatred had filled me to my very soul. Some of it lingered still. Unsettled by the experience, I thought of telling Fleet, but decided against it. I needed to hold on to the good in me, no matter what. Verbalizing the phenomenon would only make it real, and that was the last thing I wanted. I wondered how the Pures were able to resist the high.

"So why don't the Pures like to use their powers?"

"Stone and Caris believed, in our time that is, that tapping into our energy interfered too much with the human world. We only called on what we could do to help or aid when circumstances required us to intervene. I imagine the Pures of this time, Colleen and her people, feel the same way."

"I see," I muttered. "And the Tainted?"

"Tavion and his cronies used their powers all the time. They were obsessed with it and believed their calling was to purge the earth of whomever and whatever threatened it. Mainly, humankind."

"So our families believe that in this time?"

"Seems so."

I tucked my hands between my legs, as if hiding the deadly weapons would make me feel normal. "Do you know why I was taken to that underground room? And what Stone meant when he said we could've been killed if the Pures had laid hands on me?"

He stretched out his legs and rubbed his forehead. "I have no idea; though I'm sure it will come back to me."

Cracks in the log walls allowed the cold air to seep in. I reached for my shawl to pull it tighter around me, but realized it was gone. It must've fallen off in the woods during the attack. Fleet noticed my shivering and approached the fireplace. He sent his gray colored energy stream at the logs within. A small fire ignited.

"Your power is gray," I said. "Mine is white. So is Farrell's. My Dad's is… I can't remember…"

"Silver. His is silver. Your mom's is gold."

"Whose is blue then? I keep seeing vapors of blue in my mind, and I don't know why."

Fleet leaned forward. "Blue," he mumbled. "Whose energy stream is blue?" He bounced his leg up and down. "I can see it too, but I can't—Trent! Trent's is blue!"

"Yes," I half-whispered, wondering who exactly Trent was. "Trent's is blue. Like his eyes." My drifting mind seemed lost, as if wandering through an endless maze. Pieces of me were scattered. Memories of loved ones out of reach. "I am not from this time," I said softly. "I am from…" Places I knew faded from my memory banks. Things I had done unremembered.

Facing Fleet, I detected blankness in his expression, a look that must've been on me as well. He was as adrift as me. Lost in a time and space we didn't know. Pulling my hands out from under me, I opened my palms and studied them. A thin, white line laced across my right palm. I traced the scar with my fingertips, when a memory exploded in my head. I was in a red desert inside a giant dome of vapor. Tavion had me clutched by the throat and lifted off the ground. I remembered struggling for air. Blood poured from a gash in my hand. Trent and Farrell were slamming their fists against the sizzling haze, yelling at me to fight. The memory jolted me to my feet. "We have to fight what is happening to us, Fleet. No matter what. We can't let ourselves be taken by the Tainted."

A glimmer of hope sparked in Fleet's dark eyes. "You're right. We need to fight this and find Trent. We can't forget we are the good guys."

"Yeah," I said, renewed with hope. "We can't."

"I am the good guy," Fleet said again, but this time

he looked confused and startled. Then he smiled wide. "Holy shit, I am one of the good guys!"

"Huh?"

"I am remembering more of this time, and I am a Pure! Like in our original time when I was a spy in the Tainted camp, it's the same in this reality, too!"

"You're a spy? You're a spy!" I could have grabbed him and kissed him, but then I thought of Trent. But why would I think of Trent? The traveler from Texas? I sank back down to my seat. "I'm forgetting things at a rapid pace, and it's scaring the hell out of me."

Fleet pulled me to my feet and led me to the kitchen table. "Let's go over the facts of who we are. If we keep reminding ourselves of our true identities, then maybe we won't forget."

"Yes," I said, willing to believe in any method to hold on to my sanity. "Let's do that."

Fleet leaned in. "You, me, and Trent are from the future. We are Pures. Colleen and her group are Pures in this time. Stone and his group are Tainted in this time. We need to find Trent because he can help us. He's the only one not from this time, so his memories should be intact."

I repeated the facts a few times. "Got it, but I don't think it will last. Words are easy to repeat, but hard to remember." Looking far off, I said, "It's like sand sifting through my fingers, I can't hold the information."

Fleet got up and paced the room, inspecting every piece of furniture as if looking for something. "What are you doing?" I asked.

He went into the downstairs bedroom and started

fumbling around. "There must be something around here to write with."

"Great idea!" I joined him in his search. "We can write everything down and reference what we wrote when we start forgetting."

"Exactly," he added.

I climbed up the crude, wooden ladder to the loft. The only things up there were a twin-size mattress on the ground and a side table. The table had a small drawer. When I pulled it open, I found pieces of thick paper and a small brown pencil. "Got it!"

Making my way down the ladder, Fleet and I went back to the table. Holding the tiny pencil in my hand, I placed the tip on the parchment. Facts muddled my brain. *I am a Pure. No, I am a Tainted. I am not from here. I have to find…* A lump lodged in my throat and stuck there. The pencil dropped from my hand and rolled across the table. "I can't remember."

Looking at Fleet to rescue me from my forgetfulness, I saw confusion on his face. "I can't either." He slapped his hand on the pencil to prevent it from falling to the ground and handed it back to me.

"You have to," I whispered, realizing we were lost if he couldn't remember. "Come on, Fleet. Think."

"We…" He stopped for a few seconds before continuing. He pressed his hands against his forehead. He strained his face. His words came out slow and deliberate. "We are from the future." I scribbled his words, as if in a race to beat the hands of time themselves. "We are the Pure," he continued. "We need to find…"

I kept the pencil on the paper, waiting for him to finish his sentence, but he didn't. Eyeing what I had written, I noticed a ring on my finger. Two hearts joined together at the middle. I wondered how I had acquired the treasure, when Fleet blurted out, "Trent! He gave you that ring. We need to find him."

Before the name could slip either of our minds, I wrote it down. I read the message out loud. "We are from the future. We are the Pure. We need to find Trent."

A panicky stillness filled the four walls because the message seemed unfinished. "Is there more?" I asked Fleet. "This can't be it."

"I know," Fleet offered. "Let's sign the paper."

Taking the pencil in turn, we signed our names below the message. "There," I said. "Perfect."

Fleet's eyes went wide with dawning recognition. "Dominique, I am remembering something about you. You're a super conductor."

"That's right," I added. "I have immense power, and can rage out if I'm not careful." I sat up. "And if someone touches me while we are both using our power, the surge will be catastrophic. That's what my mom meant when she said she was glad no one had touched me."

"And why Farrell ushered you away to that underground room," Fleet added. He ran his hands through his thick, dark hair. "I can't recall anything else. Everything is jumbled in my head. Our identities, our purpose, things we have done and need to do, it's all mixed up." He searched my eyes with a look of desperation and sadness. "The only thing I know to be true at this moment is my love for you."

Pushing the paper aside, I placed my hand on Fleet's. "Me too. And my exhaustion. I know that to be real," I said, trying to lighten the somber mood, yet feeling unsure of everything.

Fleet smiled. He rose to his feet. "Let's rest for the night, then."

Lying beside Fleet, the vast feeling of doubt and confusion crowding my mind started giving way to the fatigue that had settled in my bones. Whatever worries we had would be better in the morning.

~INFINITI~

HOLY SHIT, DOMINIQUE HAS POWERS! STANDING IN THE woods watching her bad ass self flinging out blasts of energy from her hands had me trippin'! But when it was all said and done, and Dominique and Fleet retreated to one of the cabins, I freaked for another reason.

Fleet couldn't hear me anymore.

"Hey, Fleet!" I yelled in his ear. No response. I stood in front of the fireplace and did jumping jacks, like an idiot. Again, no flicker of detection from Fleet at all. Getting pissed, I tried banging on the wall, but ended up flinging my ghostly self through the thick logs.

Staggering out in the woods, I managed to catch my balance. I peered at the quiet cabin, not knowing how to handle the situation. "This is bad."

I was thinking of drifting my way through time and space to look for Jan and Abigail to ask for help, when I spotted Stone, Caris, and Farrell in the distance. They huddled together in a circle, having some sort of secret meeting.

"Oh, hell no," I said, zipping over to eavesdrop.

"Good idea, sending them to the cabin," Stone said to Caris. "Now we can talk without being overheard."

The three appeared confused, especially Caris. Worry lines marked her forehead and eyes.

"So, what do you all make of their strange behavior?" Stone asked the group.

Farrell rubbed his chin. "I'm not sure."

"It's almost as if they are not themselves," Caris said.

"Well, we know that," Stone replied.

"That is not what I am talking about," Caris explained. "I mean it in the literal sense. They are *really* not themselves."

Stone turned to face her. "Are you saying you think them taken over by the Pures?"

"Infiltrated at the core?" Farrell asked.

Caris shook her head, as if trying to make sense of her own words. "I don't know. But I can tell you, without a doubt, Dominique and Fleet should know things they do not know."

"Oh no," I whispered, thinking the evil crew before me was beginning to realize something was up with Dominique and Fleet, though I doubted they'd ever imagine the time travelling truth. I lifted my fingers to my mouth so I could chew my nails, but remembered I didn't have nails. Or a mouth. Ugh.

"Dominique didn't seem to know the location of the outhouse" Caris went on. "And when she set out in the night, she took my shawl instead of hers, and forgot her lamp."

Stone wagged his finger, as if remember something. "Now that you mention it, Fleet didn't know how to light the torches around the camp. I had to remind him."

"See?" Caris said. "It is not my imagination."

Stone crossed his arms. "I was also quite surprised when Dominique suggested we not seek retribution for the murder of Tavion."

"I know," Caris added. "She and Tavion were so close. I was stunned when she said that."

The three moved in even closer. Their dark eyes brimmed with distrust and suspicion. The only thing missing from their evil gathering was a five pointed star and a circle traced on the ground.

"You were alone with Dominique in the cellar," Stone said to Farrell. "Did she exhibit any unusual behavior? Say anything out of the ordinary?"

Farrell's eyes darted back and forth. "She seemed a bit tired, but otherwise her normal self."

Everything I had learned in my Psychology AP class about body language came back to me. A telltale sign for lying was shifting eyes. "You are so full of it," I said to Farrell, floating in front of him and getting up close to his super gorgeous face. "Hot, but full of it. Question is, why would you lie?"

Stone uncrossed his arms. "If something has happened to Dominique and Fleet, then it is up to us to figure it out."

Farrell moved in even closer. He lowered his voice. "What if what is happening to them is of their doing? Then what?"

"What do you mean?" Stone asked.

"I mean, what if they have switched sides," he stopped, as if afraid to finish his sentence but did anyway. "...On their own."

Stone furrowed his brow. He leveled Farrell with a death glare. "You think my daughter would betray us? Voluntarily? Never. Furthermore, I will not tolerate such blasphemy! Dominique would never turn against us." He rammed his finger against Farrell's chest. "If I hear you suggest something like that again, you will sorely regret it. Understood?"

"Oh hell, you are a baddie," I said to Stone, remembering how he was a super nice dad in my time. Now he was downright terrifying.

"Yes, sir," Farrell said sheepishly.

Stone let out a deep breath, as if calming himself. "If the Pures are hatching a plan against us and using Dominique and Fleet in some way, then we must figure it out. We must keep a watchful eye on the pair."

Finished with his cloak and dagger meeting, Stone wrapped his arm around Caris. Together they walked to their cabin. If I didn't know better, I'd say they looked like regular parents worried about their kid, not two supernatural evil beings. Farrell retreated to his cabin, too, leaving me alone in the dark.

How the heck could everything be so different in this time period? I wracked my brain trying to make sense of it all, when a realization dawned on me. Coming here had created an entirely different time line where everything was way different. "Bizarro world," I whispered.

While everyone found peace and comfort in their

slumber, I roamed the woods, shrouded in fear and self-doubt. It was my dumb idea to come here, and now everything was a colossal mess. Making my way down to the river, I hovered by the water. The multi-colored leaves from the October trees piled the river banks. Lifting my face, I took in a deep breath, but couldn't smell anything because I was dead. Of course, I knew I wasn't alive, but every time I thought of being dead, anger and depression overcame me.

"I'm so stupid," I said between ghostly sobs and invisible tears. "Stupid."

Drifting along the riverbank, alone in my misery, I heard a rustling of leaves. Was someone out there in the woods? Not wanting to be spotted, I crouched down, but then remembered no one could see me. "See?' I whispered to myself. "Stupid!"

Standing upright, I peered at the brush, waiting for whoever was out there to show themselves. A small gray cat emerged. Purring, it circled my feet. "Hey, little dude. Can you see me?" It continued moving around me, as if answering my question. "Cool, I could use a friend right about now."

I sat on the ground and let my new friend walk around me. He, or she, purred with delight, flicking its tail back and forth. "I wish I could pet you."

The cat stopped. It stared at me with big, blue eyes. The color made me think of Trent. Colleen had whisked him away in a flash of green. That was it! Trent! I needed to find him. Maybe I could somehow get through to him. He was, after all, from a family who could sense things and read auras. The mental image of his great grand-mother running an egg over Dominique's body to draw out the evil within her sprang to mind. If his ancestor we had visited from the past could do that, then surely I could communicate with Trent somehow, right? I reached out to pet my new friend, but my transparent hand moved right through it. "Thanks for the idea."

Closing my eyes, I pictured Trent. His bright blue eyes, his tan skin, how cute he and Dominique were together, how great of a guy he was. *Where are you, Trent?* My vaporous form starting whooshing through the air. Skimming the ground, I traveled along the riverbank for a while, whizzed to the other side of the slow moving stream, and stopped before a two-story log cabin. It reminded me of Richard and Sue's cabin from my time, but smaller.

Creeping my way in, I roamed the house. Trent huddled fast asleep on the floor in a pile of blankets by the fireplace. Upstairs, Colleen slept in a room by herself. Richard and Sue cuddled in slumber in another room, and the guy Dominique had attacked slept in a separate room.

I drifted back to where Trent was. "I'll wait here, I guess."

TIME HAD NO REAL MEANING FOR ME, AND BEFORE I knew it, the house started bustling with activity. Soft light streamed in through the windows. Birds started chirping outside. Richard fired up a black, bulky stove and started boiling water in an oversized teapot. Colleen and Sue joined him.

"What do you make of that kid?" Richard asked

Colleen, ticking his chin in Trent's direction. "Do you think he can do that stuff he said?'

Colleen set out a row of white coffee mugs. "Yes, I think he most certainly can."

Sue popped opened a tin can. She poured coffee beans into a brown rectangular box with a handle at the top. She started cranking the handle. "I believe in him, too."

After rotating the apparatus for a while, Sue opened a drawer at the base of the box. Craning my neck, I looked over her shoulder and saw dark powdery grinds. "Cool," I said, thinking that was the freshest ground coffee I'd ever seen.

"So we present him to be marked, and then we attack and let him do his thing?" Richard asked. He glanced over at Trent's sleeping body. "I'm happy to have him here to help us in our mission, but I feel bad about offering him to the wolves. He has no role in our quarrel with the Tainted, at least not in this time."

"Wait a damned second," I interjected. "You're gonna present Trent to be what?" Looking in his direction and shaking my head, I asked, "What the hell did you do?"

"Not so," Colleen said in answer to Richard. "His role is probably deeper than any of ours. He is connected to Dominique, and she is our biggest threat."

My mouth fell open. "Dominique is what?" I snapped my fingers in front of Colleen's face. "What do you mean Dominique is your biggest threat? I need answers people."

Sue set a strainer over a pitcher, placed the granules in it, and then poured the hot water from the pot through the strainer. "I bet that's so good," I said, taking a big whiff and wishing I could smell the delicious looking brown liquid.

Sue filled the mugs with coffee. "True, his role may be significant in his time, but their connectedness does not exist for us."

Colleen wrapped her hands around her mug. "Everything overlaps in some way or another. Time is the indefinite and collected continued progress of existence. Events in the past, present, and future are regarded as a whole. Are they not?"

"Say what?" I asked, my mouth hanging open as I tried to make sense of her philosophical mumbo jumbo.

"I suppose," Richard said, taking a gulp of brew. "But let us talk about what is truly important here."

"His power?" Colleen asked.

"Yes, indeed. He is brimming with it," Sue said. "His glow is all around him. I imagine that is why Stone and the others had him bound."

Peering at Sue, I asked, "Are y'all talking about his aura? If so, then you're right. He's loaded with powers. He's even a Supreme-whatever-human."

"We need to understand it more," Richard offered.

"Understand what?" The guy with longer hair asked, coming down the stairs.

"Good morning, Max," Richard said. "We were discussing time, connectedness, and power."

Max yawned. "Sounds boring." He poured himself a cup of coffee.

Making a mental note of his name, I got up close to study his face and realized he was Richard and Sue's kid. "Bizarro world," I uttered, knowing they didn't have kids in my time. "And also hot. What is it with y'all being so hot?"

Trent finally arose, and joined the group in the kitchen. "Good morning," he said, still looking out of place in his twenty-first-century attire. Sue handed him a cup of coffee. He took a few sips, and then looked around the room. "I guess the bathroom is outside?"

"Yes," Richard answered. "If you mean the outhouse, it is out the back door and straight ahead. You can't miss it. Take my coat hanging by the door."

"Yeah, the outhouse," Trent said correcting himself. "Thanks."

Slipping on the plain brown coat, Trent went outside and I followed. Of course I couldn't feel the temperature, but I could tell it was cold by the frost that sprinkled the grass and the puffs of air that came out of Trent's mouth. In the daylight, it was easy to spot the outhouse not far in the distance.

"Great," Trent muttered to himself.

"Yeah, that's gotta be gross," I said to him. "Good luck in there."

Giving him some privacy, I waited for him to do what he needed to do. Scanning the area and taking in the surroundings, a meow sounded. The same gray cat with blue eyes came out of the bushes and trotted over to me. "Hey, little dude! You found me!" It started circling my legs and purring with joy.

Trent emerged from the outhouse and walked my way. He studied the cat as it sauntered around me. He crouched down. "Do you see something, little cat?"

Oh my God! Yes! I knew Trent's connection to the spiritual world from his grandmother wouldn't fail me. I jumped up and down, waving my arms. "Trent! It's me! Infiniti!" The cat almost mirrored my moves, prancing and purring with excitement.

Trent stood slowly, examining the spot I inhabited. He narrowed his eyes. "Is there someone there?" He reached out and swept his arm right through me. "Infiniti? Is that you?"

Shimmery tears of joy sprang to my eyes. He may not have been able to see me, but he knew it was me! "Yes! Trent! I'm right here!"

"Infiniti, if that's you," he stopped and rubbed his chin, thinking of what to say. "Make this cat walk over to the outhouse and back."

Sighing with relief and feeling confident, I said, "I can do that. Come on, little dude. Let's show him what we got." I started walking, beckoning the cat to follow me. With my new best friend at my heels, we walked to the outhouse, then back to Trent. Standing in front of him, brimming with nervous anticipation, I waited for him to say something.

His expression shifted from doubt to belief. "Infiniti!"

The back door of the house banged open. "Trent," Richard called out. "You okay?'

Trent raised his hand. "All good!"

Richard went back inside, leaving me and Trent alone again. "Infiniti," Trent whispered. "I'm pretty sure you're here, and I have no idea how long you've been around, but I need to catch you up to speed."

I huddled in, ready to hear his plan, because everything sucked.

"Colleen and her people are the Pures," he said.

"Stone and the others are the Tainted. Tavion is dead."

"I know," I answered, even though he couldn't hear me. "So what's the plan? I say we get back to Dominique and Fleet and get back to our time. Cut our losses," I said in a rush, willing him to say the same thing. "Right?"

"I'm staying here," he said. "Colleen is going to present me as the one to be marked, and when they do, I'm going to perform the *limpia* on them, Transhuman-style."

I may have been dead, but an icy chill spread through my ghostly self anyway. So this was what they had been discussing inside when they were preparing coffee. "Not just no, but hell no!" I got up in Trent's face and pointed at him. "They will kill you! And probably Dominique and Fleet, too! Do you hear me?" I stomped my feet in rapid succession. Little dude didn't like my outburst one bit. He let out an angry hiss and swiped his paw.

Trent sighed at the cat's behavior. "I knew you wouldn't like it, but you need to get through to Fleet and Dominique. Warn them about what's going to happen if you can. It's the only way to make sure Dominique, hell, all of us, are safe." He hung his head low. "I know it wasn't the way we had planned to rewrite history, but it'll still work. Everyone will be saved. And hopefully, when it's all said and done, we can get back home."

I wanted to shake him and talk him out of his hairbrained idea, but I could tell by the stubborn look in his eye that he had made up his mind.

"If you're cursing me out right now and telling me

to come up with another solution, then stop. There is no other way."

I wasn't cursing, but should've been. He wanted to offer himself to the Tainted and take them on? Had he lost his freakin' mind? Sure it might accomplish our ultimate goal, but what if it didn't? What if he was killed instead? I had spent enough time with Dominique's dad to know he was no joke.

"I'm going now," he said. "Please, get through to Fleet and Dominique somehow. I'm counting on you to not let me down."

Great! He was playing the guilt card on me. Who the hell did he think he was? Leaving me with my furry friend, he went back to the cabin.

Slumping to the ground, I sat and thought. Should I do as Trent asked and go back to Fleet and Dominique and try to get through to them? Or should I stay here and figure out another solution to get out of this mess? I had no idea. All I knew for sure was coming to first life was the biggest mistake ever.

~ FLEET ~

A soft hand rubbed my back, made its way up to my hairline, and tickled me. "Good morning," Dominique said.

Awake already for hours, I had been struggling in silence to recall the haunting dreams that plagued my night, but couldn't. The only thing I could remember was darkness—deep, desperate, inescapable darkness. Shrugging off the desolate feeling, I rolled over to face my love. Even though her eyes carried signs of fatigue, she was still the most beautiful woman I had ever seen. I thought of asking her if she had been visited by dark dreams too, but didn't. Dominique didn't favor exposing her feelings to me, or to anyone.

"Is it morning already?" I asked with a groan. "I'm more tired than usual and long for more slumber."

"I know," she said, tracing my jaw line with her fingertips. "I'm tired, too. But the camp is bustling, and we should join the others."

She started climbing out of bed, but I pulled her back down. "Have you thought about my proposition?" I had been asking her to take off with me for months. Eventually, I hoped she would say yes, and it seemed as if she might. Her eyes would light up when I painted a life apart from the others. She had even joined me in fantasizing about our own home. We wanted a cottage nestled under the mountains near a brook or a stream. All we needed to do was leave. But then Tavion was killed, and everything changed. Her uncle's death pulled her away from our dream and closer to the Tainted, yet still I kept asking if she would leave with me.

"I've thought long and hard," she said, looking away from me. "And I can't go."

"Dominique," I pleaded. "We can be happy together. No conflict, no war, no death. Surely a life like that appeals to you."

"I know you keep asking, Fleet. But I can't abandon the cause. It is our duty to protect this world. We can't turn our backs on our purpose, especially now with Tavion gone and his impending retribution." Her eyes met mine. "If you should choose to go, I will not stand in your way."

Stubborn and defiant, she would not be swayed even by love. "I'm not leaving you." Swinging my legs over the bed and getting up, I wondered how I could continue protecting someone I loved who supported the Tainted when my job was to betray them. "I will fetch us some water."

When Colleen converted me to the Pures, Dominique and I were only friends. Over the years, a true and deep affection blossomed between us. We planned to wed, but had not yet set a date. Colleen and the others thought my connection to Dominique merely part of my ruse. I could never tell them the truth, so instead tried to convince Dominique to run off with me. The thought of the two of us being on our own and not connected to the Tainted or the Pures had once filled me with hope, but ever since the Pures took out Tavion, the idea of independence for the two of us had faded to oblivion. Dominique fully embraced the belief of the Tainted serving as the ultimate protectors of the Earth, and now demanded revenge against the Pures for their deadly actions. There was nothing I could do but stay true to who I was no matter how hard. Eventually, everything would be coming to a head and Dominique would soon know that I was infiltrating her group.

Pulling on my work clothes, I made my way to the kitchen to grab a basin. A piece of paper on the table caught my eye. I picked it up and read the message.

We are from the future. We are the Pure. We need to find Trent.

Dominique, Fleet

My hands shook. My heart slammed against my chest. *What in the hell?* I kept the paper close and glanced over my shoulder to make sure Dominique couldn't see me. Moving away from view, I read the message a few more times. The handwriting was Dominique's. Our signatures were authentic. But we were not the authors. Gritting my teeth, I scanned the room for signs of entry, but found none. Folding the parchment, I shoved it in my pocket and grabbed the large basin from the shelf.

"I'll be right back," I called out, leaving the cabin and marching down to the river.

Muttering a quick greeting to Stone and Farrell

who were tending to the horses, I made my way to the river at a fast pace. I set the basin on the ground, looked around to make sure no one was near, and pulled the note from my pocket. This time I read the words out loud, as if saying them would unlock a hidden memory. "We are from the future. We are the Pure. We need to find Trent."

I ran my thumbs over the rough parchment. I was with Dominique all night. The note was not there when we retired, so someone must've crept in while we slept. If so, who? And how did that person replicate Dominique's handwriting and our signatures? And why mention the traveler from Texas?

"Brother," Farrell said.

My fingers clamped around the note as I shoved it back in my pocket. "Blazes, Farrell. You cannot sneak up on me like that."

"I was not sneaking." He came closer. He eyed my now empty hand. "What are you up to?"

Up to? Was he asking me as part of a casual conversation? Or had he seen the paper in my hand and was accusing me of something? "Nothing. You?"

Farrell kept a laser stare on me. "I came down here to check on you." He gave a long pause. "You and Dominique were acting quite strangely yesterday. I couldn't make sense of it, and neither could the others. They asked me not to say anything. I said I wouldn't, but we are close. There are no secrets between us."

No secrets between us? How I wished that was the case and that Farrell would join me as a Pure, but every subtle suggestion I had made about turning was met with sharp reproach.

"Is there anything you want to tell me? Did something happen to you and Dominique yesterday?"

The events of yesterday swirled in my head like a churning fog. Everything I had said and done muddled my brain, as if yesterday had been clouded over by a thick storm. Had someone done something to me? Had one of the Tainted found me out and was now playing tricks with me? A twinge of panic struck my gut. Masking my alarm, I focused instead on the events of the day. "I remember walking into camp with Dominique and a traveler."

"You said his name was Trent, and that he was from Texas. You said he was a friend, though you had never mentioned him before. You and Dominique were adamant in vouching for him."

The thick fog of yesterday started to dissipate. "That's right. I'm remembering it now. We met up with him and brought him to the camp for a stay." I could not bring to mind where I had met the traveler or any circumstances regarding our acquaintance. I wondered if Dominique could.

Farrell eyed me with suspicion mixed with concern. "What else do you recall?"

My gaze traveled down the stream as I struggled to place yesterday's events in order. The constant flow of the brook sent a peaceful trickle into the cold air, calming me so I could think. "When we came into the camp, you all attacked Trent and put him in the holding cabin. Later, Colleen and her people came. They agreed to mark one of their own in retribution for what was done to Tavion. They returned in the night and took Trent." My stare settled back on Farrell. "That's all I remember."

"You don't remember acting strangely? Telling me in the cellar you'd explain things later? Even Dominique was not herself."

"No," I said. "Brother, my mind is clear now, though yesterday it was, admittedly, different." I shook my head, as if shaking the cobwebs within. "I can't explain it, but I'm fine now. I assure you."

Farrell put his hand on my shoulder. "Good. I was worried. I feared Colleen had influenced you somehow."

If Farrell knew the truth, he'd strike me dead on the spot. Colleen had indeed influenced me, but that was years ago. Every moment of my first encounter with her stayed fresh in mind.

Dominique, Farrell, and I had stumbled upon a Union field hospital while out riding one day. We called on Tavion, Stone, and Caris to join us and inspect the area. Bodies covered the grassy plain. Soldiers lay bloodied and injured next to corpses that had begun to rot. White tents were erected nearby for surgeries and other life-saving procedures for those still alive. The hollering from within those tents chilled me to the bone. Tavion's eyes brimmed with hate as he examined the scene. "Let us do them a favor and finish them off," he said.

The idea of eliminating war, famine, and other manmade disasters from the world by ridding it of the plague known as humankind had once spurred me. But shrouded in the woods, studying the down-trodden and broken men before me, I found I couldn't attack. No matter how wrong the war was, no matter how vile some humans could be, I began to see how wrong it was to intervene. If these men had survived a battle, then who were we to take that from them?

"Perhaps we should let them be," I suggested.

Tavion leveled me with a deadly glare. He pointed to the camp. "They are monsters, and it is our duty to rid this world of monsters."

Scanning the faces of my companions, searching for a shred of support, I found none. They were either sold on Tavion's deadly theory, or too afraid to speak. I was alone in my quiet rebellion, so kept my tongue.

"We will spread out and encircle the camp," Tavion ordered. "Blast them on my signal."

Getting into position, carefully picking a spot where I would not be seen, I crouched and waited for Tavion's sign. From my vantage point, I could see women working their way through the throng, tending to the wounded. Cries and moans carried in the wind. The stench of carnage and death wafted in the air. These men were fighting their own brothers, killing each other in an attempt to make the other bend to their will. We were no better than them. It was not right for them to take such drastic measures to win. It also was not right for us to interfere.

"It is *not* right," a strong female voice said.

Spinning around, I found myself face to face with Colleen, the leader of the Pures, the enemy of the Tainted. Tall and imposing, I found myself less ready to strike and more inclined to listen. "What is not right?"

She swept her arm. "All of it."

A black beacon shot up in the air—Tavion's signal. Gasps rang out from the field of soldiers. Eyeing them, I watched as they were bombarded by energy streams that shot at them from all corners. The vaporous onslaught incinerated the men, the women, their tents, their hopes, their fears, their dreams, their futures. Everything was gone within a few seconds, the entire area reduced to ash, and I had not partici-pated. I could not. That was when I joined Colleen and the Pures.

"Brother," Farrell said again, tearing me away from that memory. His hand still rested on my shoul-der. "You sure you are well?"

"Yes," I said with a smile. "I'm fine. And I assure you I will always be faithful to our cause." The lie rolled off my tongue with ease, but I could not shake the feeling that something was amiss with me. Thinking of the paper in my pocket, I knew for certain I needed to see Colleen and the traveler named Trent. Everything changed when he appeared, so perhaps he had answers.

Picking up the basin, I knelt and dipped it into the cold river. The clear liquid sloshed as I lifted it full. "You can tell the others I am well, as is Dominique."

Farrell gave a nod. "I will."

Back in the cabin, I found Dominique fully dressed and ready for the day. She had set out some bread and fruit on the table. "That took you long enough."

"I know. I saw Farrell at the river bank. We were talking."

"About what?"

If Farrell thought I was acting strange yesterday, did Dominique think the same thing? I had been a part of the group for so long now, hiding my true association, sure of my cover, but had I blown it somehow? Were they onto me? I shrugged. "Nothing important."

The note felt like a piece of lead in my pocket, weighing me down with doubt and uncertainty. I set the basin on the counter. Dominique came up behind me and slipped her arms around my waist. She rested her head against my back.

"It has been so nice being here with you. Alone, the two of us."

My spirits lifted. Had she changed her mind? Was she finally ready to strike out with me and leave the Pures and the Tainted behind us? I turned and cupped her face in my hands. "What are you saying?"

"I am saying we wed and strike out on our own, *after* we end this feud."

My hands dropped from her face. I cast my eyes down. I knew exactly what she was saying, but asked anyway. "How do we end the feud?"

She took my hands and squeezed. "We avenge Tavion and kill the Pures. Once we end them, we can be together, you and I. Forever."

"But we have asked for them to mark only one. Stone and Caris agreed to this."

"Forget what my parents want. When the Pures offer up their marked one, you and I will strike. Your power combined with mine can eliminate them."

"And if they should touch you? Channel your strength and use it against us?"

"They will not know what is happening until it is too late. No one will touch me."

Keep her in exchange for the lives of the Pures? I couldn't do it. No love could spur me to kill like that.

"Okay," I muttered. "We do things your way, and then we leave."

Finishing our breakfast and joining the others, my brain started formulating a plan. I needed to get to Colleen and the others as soon as possible. The traveler from Texas was key in what was happening. I needed to find him and talk to him before Dominique killed every last one of them.

~TRENT~

GOING BACK INTO THE CABIN, I WONDERED IF INFINITI would be able to get through to Dominique and Fleet. With everything going horribly wrong for us since arriving here, I doubted it. I also couldn't help but think I was destined to die here.

"Hey, Trent," Max said with a laugh. "Did you lose your way out there?"

I thought of being lost from everyone I loved, stuck in a place and time that didn't belong to me. "I've most definitely lost my way," I said, sitting by the fireplace.

"Uh, sorry," Max offered, catching on to how miserable I was. "I was only joking with you."

"It's fine," I mumbled, studying the tongues of flames. A deep ache settled in my heart. Grief over my inevitable death consumed me. What if my plan didn't work? What if Stone and the others overtook us and actually marked me? Being marked meant being hunted for lifetimes. I had seen it firsthand with Dominique. Although I'd be glad to take that burden from her and our future child, or anyone's child, it wasn't a fate I wanted.

A hand lighted on my shoulder. It was Colleen. She handed me my coffee. "We won't let you fail."

I tilted my head and studied her green eyes and fair complexion. "Can you read minds or something?"

"I don't have to read minds to see the doubt written on your face."

I hated being so down, but couldn't help myself. I missed my house, my *Abuela*, my college, and most importantly, the love of my life. I thought of how Jan and Abigail had shown us the moment we discovered our son's mark. The pain had cut deep. Sure we were here and timelines were different now, but the Tainted were nothing but evil. If not my son, then someone else's would be at risk. I refused to let other innocents suffer like that. My *limpia* had to work. If it didn't, we needed an alternate plan.

The others filed in around me. Together now, as if Colleen had called a meeting to order, I set my mug down and voiced what I didn't want to admit. "If I fail, and the *limpia* doesn't work, we're gonna need a Plan B, or a Hail Mary."

"A plan what? And you want us to pray?" Max blurted with a confused look on his face.

"Sorry, they're expressions from my time." I scooted to the edge of my seat to explain. "A plan B is a plan that's initiated once an original plan fails. A Hail Mary is a crazy long pass into the end zone when a football team is losing a game and the clock's about to run."

Richard scratched his head. "I get the first part, but not the second part."

"His word choice is unimportant," Colleen interjected. "Our guest is saying we need a plan should the *limpia* not work. Is that correct, Trent?"

"Yes, exactly. We need to be prepared for the worst." No one spoke. Even the crackling flames from the fire seemed to silence as everyone considered the possibility of failing.

Max formed a fist. "I've wanted to fight the Tainted for years."

A look of inevitability darkened Colleen's face. "The future has collided with the past. Your arrival here has shown me there is no compromising. While violence is not our way, I believe it is us or them at this point. If all else fails, maybe we should change our ways this one time. Maybe we should fight."

Petite in stature, Sue looked up at Richard. As if giving in to an old argument, she echoed, "Maybe we should."

Richard gave a solemn nod. "It may be time to do something different."

Staring at my green-eyed hosts, realizing they had agreed to something they had probably debated for years, I wondered if they fully grasped what they were getting into. I had seen the horror of the Tainted. They had tracked down Dominique for nine lifetimes. Although we were in some sort of alternate reality, we were still in first life. The Pures in my time hadn't been able to defeat the Tainted until life nine. Could this first attempt at defeating the Tainted turn out differently? "Okay," I said, willing to try anything. "How do we fight them?"

"Let us figure this out together, starting with you," Colleen offered. "You are overflowing with energy. Explain that to us."

I had told them the entire saga of what Dominique and I had been through, but had failed to mention I was a Supreme Transhuman. "Oh yeah, that," I said. "Well, for starters, I'm a Supreme."

Richard smiled wide. He reached over and punched Max on the shoulders. "I told you there was something special about Trent Avila."

Sue's mouth fell open. "So that is how you were able to call to us. We should have known."

"How could we have known? Until this young man arrived, we thought Supremes were extinct." Colleen moved about the room, tapping her finger against her temple. "We have the advantage, for once."

"Seems that way," I added, agreeing with her.

Her eyes narrowed, she took on a fierce expression. "Here's the plan, then. We go forward with offering Trent for marking. When the Tainted have him, we will tether them with our blasts. Once they are down, Trent will perform his procedure. If unable to complete the task, we will show them the biggest fight they have ever seen."

My coming here was forcing them to change their course of action. Instead of going along with marking someone, the Pures were going to strike back. "We take them out," I expanded. "But we spare Dominique and Fleet so the three of us can go home. Yes?"

"Yes." She grabbed her staff. "With that behind us, let's fight."

Max leaped to his feet. Delight spread across his face, like a kid given permission to enter a candy store. He eyed me with deadly playfulness. "Let's see what you're made of."

"Wait a minute." I rose to my feet and gave Colleen a questioning look. "You want me to fight right now?" I pointed at Max. "With him?"

She made her way to the back door. "Yes. With him. Now." She held open the door. "He won't hurt you. Right, Max?"

"I promise I will not hurt him...too badly."

Rubbing the back of my neck, unsure about the whole fight club thing, I stepped outside. Droplets of morning dew still sprinkled the grass. The cold still bit the air. I brought my hands up to my face and blew warm breath into my palms, thinking how Infiniti was going to miss the big show.

"Don't worry," Max teased. "You will warm up shortly."

Great, I thought, remembering the pain and heat I had endure while tied up in Stone's prison. Walking to the far end of the grassy air, I turned and faced my sparring partner. Max's expression had switched from playful to deadly. Colleen, Richard, and Sue stayed on the back porch, like spectators waiting for the main event to begin.

"So, how do we do this thing?"

"Like this," Max warned. He flung out his arm and shot a stream of vapor at my chest. It lodged into me, knocking me on my back with a thud.

Struggling to get air, I coughed until I could breathe again. "What the hell," I muttered, getting up and dusting myself off.

"You need to be ready to dodge or deflect," Colleen instructed from the sidelines. "Pick your strategy."

Dodge or deflect my ass. I was ready to strike. Max needed to know who he was dealing with. Getting my feet under me, I eyed my opponent, then rested my hands as I considered my move.

"Your power is an extension of yourself," Colleen called out. "Think of your energy as—"

An extension of myself... Latching on to that phrase, the remainder of her lecture droned in the background of my thoughts. I pictured my aura, pretending it was like a Roman Candle. When I was little, it was my favorite Fourth of July pyrotechnic device. I remembered gripping the base of the firework, lighting the tip, and extending it as far away from my body as possible while explosive lights rocketed into the air. *Be a Roman Candle,* I said to myself.

I threw out my arms. Blasts of blue-hued sparks careened straight for Max. He brought his arms in front of him, forming a barrier of white smoke that deflected my efforts with ease, my sapphire blast disintegrating at contact.

"Good, but you are better than that," Colleen encouraged.

Of course I knew I was better, but I couldn't get a hold of my strength. How could I control something so wild and untamed?

"Practice deflecting," Colleen directed. "Like Max."

Huffing from the exertion of my puny Roman Candle attempt, I gave her a nod. Warding off attacks would be a useful skill. Mastering a strong defense should probably come before offense anyway, at least in a fight like this. Holding out my arm, I motioned at Max to come closer. "Come at me, bro."

Max stretched his arms and popped his neck. "Bro? As in brother?"

"Yeah. Brother from another mother." I grinned, knowing the saying would go way over his head. "Give me a blast."

"Okay, then, brother from another mother. Brace yourself. I won't be holding back this time."

Crap. He'd gone easy on me before? If that was the case, then I really needed to channel my energy. Widening my stance, I centered my weight. I lifted my hands in front of me, palms facing out, and focused on blocking whatever he'd hurl my way.

He blew out. He clenched his jaw. Then, with a grunt, he blasted a wave of energy in my direction. Locking my arms, I forced my aura out of me, imagining it shaped like a shield and as strong as titanium. The onslaught shook my hands. My arms nearly buckled, yet my efforts held.

"That's it!" I heard Richard cheer. "You're doing it!"

Surprised at my ability, and wanting to impress the onlookers, I concentrated on sending the blast back. Lunging forward, I directed my aura to repel the torrent, like a reflection. I bore down. I threw my weight into my return assault. An array of blue exploded around me. Voices hollered. Everything dimmed for a few seconds.

Snapping to, I found myself on my knees. Richard had me in a bear hold from behind. His hands were clasped tight around my chest. "Are you powered down?"

"Yes," I said in a low voice. My body trembled. My knees throbbed. Heat pricked at my skin.

"I'm going to let go now," Richard cautioned.

Releasing me, I took in my bearings, realizing the horror of what I had done. The trees and brush before me had burned to a crisp. Plumes of smoke rose from the charred remains. Max knelt on all fours, struggling for breath. Ash dusted his face and clothes. Sue hovered over him, making sure he was all right.

"What did I do?" I uttered, stricken with guilt.

Colleen took my hands. She helped me up with a firm grip. "You did what I instructed you to do, and then some."

"I didn't mean to—"

Richard patted my back. "We know you didn't."

Unsure how he'd react to me, I approached Max with caution. "Max, I'm so sorry. Are you okay?"

"I am fine." He cradled his chest and stood with a groan. "See, I told you you'd warm up."

Back inside, Richard and Sue tended to Max while Colleen analyzed my performance. She called my talent raw, suggesting I rein it in if I should feel it overtaking me. She lectured me on the ins and outs of self-control and intention. While some of her words sank in, the majority didn't. I was too shocked at what I had done and scared to death that in defending my group, I'd end up hurting them. Or killing them.

The day quickly turned to night and everyone went to bed early. I searched for some sort of peace while I lay in front of the fireplace with my pillow and blankets, but found none. With sleep out of reach,

I kept replaying the image of Max's injured face and Richard and Sue's shocked eyes. After what I had done, they still believed in me and our plan. I prayed I wouldn't let them down.

Tossing and turning, the padding of footsteps reached my ears. With the soft moonlight trickling through the windows, I saw Max coming down the stairs. I propped myself up on my arms.

"Hey, Max."

"You still awake, traveler?" He headed for the kitchen, lighting a candle with a flick. He got a mug, and poured water into it from the pitcher on the shelf.

"I can't sleep." I joined him and took a seat at the table. Eying the space, I thought of my kitchen back home. Not only did I miss my *Abuela* and her cooking, but I also missed the modern conveniences of my century. "You know, in my time, kitchens have refrigerators."

"Refriger- what?"

"Re-frig-er-ators," I said nice and slow. "It's a big appliance you plug in and it keeps everything inside of it cold."

Max sipped his water. "You are speaking nonsense," he laughed. "Appliance? Plug in?"

"Yeah, it hasn't been invented yet. None of it has."

He refilled his mug, filled one for me, and sat next to me. "This time must be so odd for you."

"You have no idea."

We sat there in the quiet for a while, neither one of us knowing what to say. Max fiddled with his mug for a bit. "What is keeping you awake?"

I rubbed my face. "Oh, just that little thing called death."

He shrugged. "If we are meant to die, then we will die. If we are meant to live, then we will live. It is as simple as that."

"I suppose," I said, admiring his practical outlook because in this situation there was no use worrying about the outcome. Whatever was going to happen, was going to happen.

"Get some sleep," Max said, getting up and leaving me alone with my doubts. "And by the way, you were good with the—" He stopped to search for the right words. "Hail Holy letter B."

"Hail Mary, Plan B," I smiled.

"Yes, that. You were good with that."

He started to walk away, when I stopped him. "Max, I'm really sorry about what I did to you."

"Don't be. We know what you can do now. For the first time, I think this whole cursed feud can end, thanks to you."

Alone again, wanting to believe Max was right, I thought fresh air could do me some good. Pulling on Richard's coat, I slipped outside to clear my head. I half expected to see the gray cat that had attached to Infiniti, but didn't. *Good*, I thought. She was doing what I asked. If Infiniti could get through to Dominique and Fleet, then they could join us in our fight. But what if she couldn't reach them? If only I could deliver my message myself.

"*Dile*," the Spanish speaking voice whispered in my ear.

The hairs on my arm sprung. My body shivered. *Tell her?* Shifting around, I searched the cold outdoors. I didn't see anyone, and I wasn't expecting to because the voice was the same one I'd heard when I was imprisoned. But who was it? And how on earth did the messenger expect me to tell Dominique anything?

"*Dile*," the voice repeated with urgency.

"Fine," I said out loud, thinking I was going slightly crazy. "I'll try."

I walked further away from the cabin and sat beneath a large tree. The branches sprawled overhead, concealing me in shadow. My warm breath sent puffs of vapor into the freezing air. My face and hands started to chill. Ignoring the cold, I focused on clearing my mind and thought only of Dominique.

Her image formed clearly in my mind—long brown hair, olive-colored eyes, the sprinkle of freckles you could only see when up close. I could almost feel her soft skin, could almost taste her sweet lips. Everything inside of me became one with her, and it was as if she was with me.

Soft vibrations echoed all around me. A warm tingle covered my body. Opening my eyes, I saw my blue aura. Soft yet deep, it floated around me like a mist. "Whoa," I said, reaching out to touch the haze. "It's working." Marveling at what I could do, I said, "Show me Dominique."

The color pulsed with brightness. It gathered in front of me. An image formed in the middle. Fuzzy at first, the picture became clearer as I willed my aura to do what I wanted.

Dominique came into focus. She was walking along the riverbank. Darkness shrouded her, but I could see her white dress clearly. She twirled her hair with her hand, gazing up at the sky with a look of sadness on her face. She seemed lost and alone, like me. "Dominique," I whispered.

She stopped.

"Dominique," I said again, but louder.

She turned around. She walked closer to where I sat. "Who is there?"

My heart leapt with joy. She could hear me. "Dominique," I said again. "It's me, Trent. Can you see me?"

"Who?" She lifted her hand, forming a ball of white in her palm. She held the light out, so she could see better. "The traveler from Texas?"

A male voice called out to her. Her light faded. She dropped her hand, whisked my image away, and darted from view.

Alone again in the cold, I sat dumbfounded. Tingles of panic worked their way through my body and I shuddered. Dominique didn't recognize me.

~DOMINIQUE~

Peering out the window, I watched Fleet make his way to the river to fetch us some water. Alone in the cabin, my brain struggled to make sense of the strange feelings inside of me. A shadow loomed in my head, clouding the details of yesterday. It carried with it feelings of despair and helplessness, but why?

Slipping out of my night dress and into my day clothes, I noticed a silver ring on my finger. A wave of panic cascaded over me. *What is this?* I brought the token closer for inspection. The slim band had two joining hearts. Eying the ring, a melancholy feeling came over me, but why? A memory of me telling Mother that Fleet had given me the ring sprang to mind, though I couldn't recall the details. "What is happening to me?" I muttered. I yanked the ring off and slammed it down on the side table.

"Focus on what you know," I told myself. Closing my eyes, I forced myself to concentrate on yesterday. I remembered walking into the camp with Fleet and a traveler from Texas named Trent. Father and the others had bound him and dragged him off. Later, Colleen came and accepted the terms Father had offered for the murder of Tavion, agreeing to mark one of her own in three days. She returned later and took the traveler.

Who is he? Why did she take him?

Unable to remember much else, I started working my brush through my hair. With each stroke, glimmers of a dream I'd had last night came to me. A dark ocean. A red desert. Blood dripping from my hand. My brush tumbled out of my grasp. The images made my gut clench and filled me with fear.

Stop, I commanded myself. *It was only a dream.*

Shoving the sensations away, I thought of Fleet. He had been asking me to run away with him for a while now. The thought of he and I being alone and not affiliated with the Tainted had started to appeal to me, but that notion ended when Tavion was murdered by the Pures.

Tavion had been as close to me as my own father, sometimes even closer. I would never forget the time he and I were on a survey, scouting the land to make sure our camp remained hidden to passersby with ill intent. Our region has just begun to be settled. Humans were curious and eager, but also cold-blooded and treacherous. After a long day of travel, we decided to give the horses and ourselves a rest. We made camp for the night near a fresh stream of water.

I had been sleeping peacefully, when a body crashed down on me. A foul smelling cloth smothered my face, muffling my screams. Greedy hands lifted my skirt and started probing me. I struggled to kick my legs and wrench my arms loose, but couldn't move. There were too many hands holding me down. Thrashing about I caught glimpses of electrical blasts mixed with flashes of torch light.

"Dominique!" Tavion yelled. His shouts were reduced to muffled cries as a multitude of shots rang out.

My body stilled. My heart lurched. Had Tavion been killed?

"Atta girl," the monster on top of me had said, ripping off my undergarments. "Just stay still like that."

Gathering my rage, remembering every horror story Tavion had ever told me about humankind, I let out a piercing yell. Deadly hatred pushed out of me. A rumble shook the earth. A thunderous boom cut the air. The cloth at my face fell off, revealing my intense light. The brilliance filled my vision, drowning out everything around me. Nothing else existed but my hate and my light.

I had no idea how long I had lain there, or how long the flash had lasted, but eventually the radiance turned to darkness. I felt nothing. The night became my world. The shadows that blanketed me were my only companions.

Over time, a whisper met my ear. "Dominique." It was Tavion, crawling over to me. I could hear his body dragging across the dirt. "Dominique," he said again, between muffled sobs. He touched my face. "Are you all right?"

My throat had dried out. My lips had stuck together. Forcing them to part, I whispered, "Yes," but thought, *No.*

With the sun rising behind him, I was able to see

what the camp invaders had done to my uncle. Blood splattered his face. Bruises forced his eyes closed. His lip bulged out. He helped me up and hugged me. "My niece," he whispered. "My beautiful niece."

Wrapping my arms around him, I felt wet stickiness at his back. A cascade of sobs poured out of me. "What did they do to you?"

"They shot and stabbed me," he mumbled. "But you…you killed them. You saved us, my darling girl."

Tavion had been shot and stabbed over one hundred times. Both of us broken in every way imaginable, we found ourselves a new camp and stayed there while we healed—Tavion from his external wounds, and me from my internal ones. From then on, I knew Tavion was right. Humankind did not deserve this planet. We never told Mother, Father or the others about the incident, deciding instead to keep it to ourselves. The pain of that evening was too difficult to share, too painful to relive. It became mine and Tavion's secret.

Pushing the memory aside, I thought of Tavion. My dreams had to have been a message about him. Hell-bent on avenging my beloved uncle, I had suggested we obliterate the Pures. Father had dismissed the idea, instead settling on the death of only one. "One life for another," he had said.

Maybe my dreams were telling me to forget my father's plan and to follow through with my desires. Staring down at the fallen hairbrush, I picked it up, thinking about ending my enemies. It would accomplish what Fleet wanted while at the same time honoring my uncle. With the Pures wiped out and

Tavion avenged, I could leave the group. Fleet and I could be alone. Forever. Just the two of us.

But would Fleet agree to such a plan? He had started to go soft on humans, but maybe he would do it for me. Finished with my hair, my gaze settled back on the ring. It had to have come from Fleet. With no other plausible explanation, I placed it back on my finger.

Ready for the day, I went to the kitchen and opened the cupboard. The smell of over-ripe fruit wafted my way. The cabin sat mostly empty, so didn't have much stock for eating—a dry loaf of bread and a few overly soft apples. It would do. Cutting up the rations, I set them out on a plate. If Fleet and I were married, we could live together in our own cabin, with our own food, doing what we pleased. As of now, Fleet and I could barely even be alone. It was a huge surprise when Mother had suggested we stay the night together. A pleasant surprise, but why did she allow it?

Again, nothing about yesterday made sense.

Standing by the window, I leaned against the wall and waited for Fleet. I loved him and wanted to be with him. Would he agree to my stipulations?

Finally, Fleet came into view. His hands gripped the filled basin. The water sloshed over the sides with each stride. He looked downtrodden and burdened with a creased brow and tense shoulders. Even so, he was strikingly handsome and all mine, I longed to ease his troubles.

Coming inside, he explained that he had taken so long because he saw Farrell at the river and had gotten caught up in conversation. I thought of his brother, so faithful to Fleet and the cause, yet somewhat shrouded in mystery. What would he say if we left? I did not think he would like it.

Hugging Fleet from behind and leaning my head against his back, I said, "It has been so nice being here with you. Alone."

He turned around and cupped my face in his strong hands. "What are you saying?"

Hope filled his eyes. I could tell he wanted me to say I was ready to leave with him. Instead, I told him we needed to end the feud first and kill Colleen and the others.

His hands dropped from my face. He cast his eyes down, unable to look at me. I hated the conflict within him, but knew my way would solve our problems. Before he could lodge into any objections, I explained how we would strike during the marking ceremony. His main concern was for me, but once we got past that, he offered no further opposition. Satisfied with our course of action, and after eating, Fleet and I joined the others outside.

My parents and Farrell were eyeing the area around the bonfire. "When they arrive and offer their one, we will do the marking here," Father instructed.

We had never performed a marking before, though the ritual was well known. Subdued, the victim would lay on his or her back. The person performing the imprint would touch the victim at the base of the neck, pouring enough essence into them to render the person traceable.

Mother tapped her chin. "We'll need a platform."

Fleet stepped forward. "I can go to town and get the supplies."

Farrell patted Fleet on the back. "I will join you, Brother."

Farrell's offer to go with Fleet cast a hesitant expression across Fleet's face. It even took him a few seconds to accept his brother's company. Gazing at the others, I saw that no one else noticed the reaction. When I turned my attention back to Fleet, he purposefully avoided eye contact with me. Had I gone too far with my plan to attack the Pures? Was he changing his mind? If so, I would need to be prepared to strike alone if necessary.

While my parents continued to sort out the details regarding the platform and where it would be erected, I went with Fleet and Farrell to ready the horses. Farrell mounted his steed and trotted down to the road where he waited for me and Fleet to say our goodbyes.

With quiet unease lingering between us, I handed Fleet a sack of dried fruit. He took it and tied it to his saddle. He wrapped his arm around my waist and brought me in close. "I will be back in the morning."

"Be careful," I said. "I do not trust the town folk."

"We'll be fine." He stared into my eyes. "I love you, you know."

I could almost hear an unspoken phrase tacked to the end of his sentence, 'I love you, you know, even if you are mad.' Dismissing what he would never say, I placed my hands around his neck and brought him down so our lips could meet. "I love you, Fleet," I whispered before kissing him tenderly.

I watched as Fleet and Farrell slipped from view, the feeling of something not being right strong inside of me. After they rode off, I went back to where my parents were. Mother had gone back into the cabin, and Father was nowhere to be found. He always made me feel better, and understood my bond with Tavion like no one else. I made my way to the river and discovered him fly-fishing. His pants were rolled up to his knees. He flicked his line back and forth a few times, then cast it upstream. I sat on a boulder on the edge of the riverbank across from where he stood and waited for him to notice me.

His line drifted past my location. "Dominique," he said. "Fleet and Farrell take off okay?"

"Yes, they did."

He reeled in his line, and repeated the casting motion. "You feeling well?"

"Yes, I am well." Yesterday remained jumbled in my head, and hearing my father ask about my state of health validated my sentiment that something was wrong about that day.

Father watched his line drift past. It bobbed along, dipping in and out of the water's surface. With no bites, he reeled it in, perched the rod on his shoulder, and splashed his way over to me. He climbed out of the river and sat beside me. "Is something on your mind? You have that look about you."

He knew me so well. "I can never forgive the Pures for what they did to Uncle," I confessed, wondering how he'd react when Fleet and I attacked them at the marking. Knowing him, he'd stand beside me, then express his anger after. By then, it wouldn't matter since Fleet and I would be leaving anyway. If my plan worked, Fleet and I would be in our own place well before the first snowfall.

"Anything else?" he prodded.

The cool breeze caressed my face as I considered his question. Father and Mother knew something had happened to me and Tavion that fateful trip, but they never pressed it. We had eventually told them of a skirmish while we camped, but left out the part about Tavion being shot and stabbed multiple times over, and of those filthy hands that had violated me. "I miss Uncle," I whispered.

Father placed his hand on top of mine. "I do, too, Dominique. I do, too."

He glanced out at the water. "What about your betrothed, is all well with him?"

The cool breeze caressed my face, and I wondered why he would ask about Fleet. Father didn't ask much about my private life. "He is well."

Father picked up a rock and side-tossed it. It skipped across the water four times before plunging out of view. "Things will be much better after the marking. Trust me."

"I know," I agreed.

Father got up and dusted off the back of his pants. He adjusted his reel and went back into the water. Watching him fish, laughing with him and joking around for the remainder of the day, I started to feel like my old self. My plan to strike the Pures was the answer to so many problems. With Colleen and her group taken out, I'd finally avenge Tavion. Not only could Fleet and I get on with our lives, but so could Father and Mother and even Farrell. They did not need to spend their time worrying about me or the Pures.

The day soon turned to night. Plans were discussed, supper was had, and eventually it was time to turn in. Mother had agreed I could sleep in the guest cabin again, and I found myself comfortably alone.

Sitting by the fireplace, I watched the flames flicker and pop. So many emotions filtered through me—dread, confusion, fear. I ran my hands over my dress, when something caught on the fabric. The ring. I twirled it with my thumb and watched as the light from the fire danced across the metal. "How did Fleet give this to me?" I asked out loud, as if an explanation would somehow come to me. Finding none, I went outside so I could gather my thoughts.

Breathing in the cold air, I held my breath for a bit, and then let it trickle out of my mouth. I repeated the technique, trying to erase the strangeness within me, but couldn't. It had stuck with me like sap on a tree.

Twisting at a strand of hair, I gazed up at the sky. Fleet and I would often gaze at the stars, counting the biggest ones. Perhaps doing that would settle me.

Admiring the twinkling canvas overhead, a hushed voice carried in the wind. My body froze. Tingles of fear cascaded down my spine. The voice whispered again, but this time I heard it clearly. It was a male voice, and it was calling my name. I spun around. Before me hovered a blue mist. I inched closer to it. "Who is there?"

"It's me, Trent. Can you see me?" the voice asked.

"Who?" Letting my energy seep out of my fingertips, I fashioned a white ball of light in my hand and held it out so I could see better. The sapphire haze gathered together. An image started forming within. It was a guy with brown hair. He wore a coat and sat beneath a tree. A flicker of familiarity registered with me. A sense of knowing him in an intimate way grew in my heart and sent a flurry of butterflies in my stomach. I stepped closer to the haze. "The traveler from Texas?"

Footsteps crunched nearby. "Daughter," Father called out, approaching my area.

I dropped the light from my hand, flicked the vaporous image away, and walked briskly over to him. "Father, what are you doing out here?"

"Same as you, probably. Sleep was escaping me, so I came out here and saw your light." He glanced around. "Were you talking to someone?"

Faking a yawn, I said, "No. It is only me out here. I was having a hard time sleeping, but now I am exhausted." I stepped in the direction of the cabins.

Father continued glancing about, clearly not believing me. "See you in the morning, then."

"Yes, see you."

Back in my cabin and safely in bed, I pulled my covers up to my chin. "Trent," I said out loud, thinking of the traveler and wondering why he had contacted me. I felt as if I knew him, *really* knew him, and he most definitely appeared to know me. I tried to remember walking into the camp with him and Fleet. Where were we before? How did he join us? My mind drew a blank.

Letting out a grunt, I turned to face the wall. I forced my eyes shut. I told myself to forget the traveler. He meant nothing to me. The only thing that mattered was carrying through with my plan to eliminate the Pures.

~FLEET~

THE HORSES TROTTED AT A SLOW PACE ALONG A PATH OF flattened grass and low lying weeds and brush. The sun shone brightly on the cold, crisp day. I had volunteered to get the lumber for the platform so I could send a message to Colleen. With Farrell joining me, reaching out to the Pures would be difficult, yet I still had to try. Something about my voided memories, the note in my pocket, and the traveler from Texas told me something horribly wrong loomed in the horizon. Even Farrell sensed it. More quiet than usual, he hadn't uttered a word since we left camp.

After a bit, a gray cat emerged from the woods and started striding alongside us. It kept looking up at me in a strange fashion. "Seems we have a companion," I said to Farrell.

Farrell eyed the cat. He smiled. "Looks like the feline has taken a fancy to you. It might make a good pet for you and Dominique."

I laughed. "We are most certainly not looking for a pet." I shooed at the cat. "Get along."

The scraggly cat paused for a few seconds, but kept following us. "Suit yourself," I said to it.

We continued in silence again, enjoying the fresh air and warm sunlight of a cold day. Things used to be easy with Farrell. We understood each other perfectly, until I had switched alliances. Glancing at him, still convinced I could make him see the error of his ways, I asked, "Do you ever long for peace, Brother?"

Farrell eyed me for a few seconds before staring ahead at the path before us. "Do you remember what life was like around here in the early days?"

"Of course I do."

"Our river was called the Ottawa after the local band of Native Americans. Captain Harry Boardman came here in 1848, set up his sawmill, and acquired timber rights for the area. Everything changed after that—the river, the people, the atmosphere. It will never be the same."

I thought of stopping his lecture, but knew he needed to get it out.

"Do you remember the tribes that were aligned with the Ottawa?" he asked.

I kept quiet because it was no use for me to answer. Farrell went on. "The Ojibway and the Potawatomi, together with the Ottawa, were known as the Anishnaabek, or the Good People. Over thirty years ago, President Jackson signed the Indian Removal Policy. These tribes, along with countless others, have been and are being wiped out. Right before our very eyes. Over time, none of them will exist. We cannot sit idly by and let it happen. So to answer your question, yes, I do long for peace. The only way to have it is to intervene where others will not or cannot."

Even though everything Farrell said resonated with me, I could not reconcile the idea of taking life to save life. Like those wounded men in the field, I couldn't strike any longer. "Killing is not the answer."

Farrell stopped his horse. "Then why are you with us?"

My horse stopped, too. Sensing the tension between me and Farrell, it whinnied and stomped its hooves. "You are my brother. Dominique is my betrothed. Our group has been together a long time. I cannot abandon you all, even with my changing perspective."

"Are you sure that is the only thing that has changed? Your perspective?"

A shudder passed through me. Did he know I had joined the Pures? Or was he merely speculating? "I will not entertain what you are suggesting," I said, spurring my horse on and avoiding further confrontation.

The quiet between us returned and stayed until we entered the town. The small village had grown since my last visit. From a narrow dirt path with huts and cabins, to a widened gravel road flanked with new buildings, I didn't even know what it was called anymore. And it didn't matter. My objective was two-fold: get the timber we needed for the platform, and get a message to Colleen. With the marking in two days, failure was not an option.

We tethered our rides outside a local inn called the

Mansion House, secured ourselves a room for the night, and then set off to purchase timber. Night was starting to fall, and we needed to acquire our goods before it got too dark.

Farrell and I stayed close, skirting the few buildings that lined the main road, and avoiding interaction with people. Almost to the timber farm, a hulking figure sauntered out in front of us. Two others flanked him on either side, and the trio blocked our path.

Big and bulky, and seeming to be the leader, the one in the middle ticked his chin at us. "God's wounds, there is sumthin' not right with you two and your people." He eyed us with disdain. "You don't show yourselves 'round here much, and when you do, there's no sign of aging. It ain't right."

"What in the sane hell are ya?" another guy asked from behind. The three before us had been joined by two behind us.

I raised my hands slightly. "We have no quarrel with you. Let us pass."

The leader smiled, exposing a row of brown and decayed teeth. "An' if we don't?"

Farrell sidled around to face the two thugs at the rear, standing back to back with me. "Well," Farrell said, "if you don't, then we will have to make you."

A crowd gathered in the middle of the road. They taunted us to fight with jeers and hollering. Encouraged by the show of support, the three started opening and closing their hands. They shifted in their boots.

"Don't hurt them," I whispered to Farrell.

The oversized leader laughed. "He is worried 'bout hurting us!" He punched his thick fist into his other hand. He licked his lips. Rocking on his feat, ready to pounce, I knew he'd be the first one at me. The other two stayed one step behind—they'd only move if he did. "The ones getting hurt are you two. Get 'em, boys!"

The leader rushed me, the other two followed. With a throat jab at the brute in the middle, I grabbed the other two and slammed them together. They crashed to the floor with a thud. Two clunks behind me told me Farrell had easily handled his attackers as well.

"Hey!" an angry voice shouted from the road. A bearded man dressed in overalls pointed a rifle at me and Farrell. He cocked his weapon. The crowd around him scattered. "Them there's my friends!"

"Son of a bitch," I muttered.

"We need to strike," Farrell urged.

Standing shoulder to shoulder with Farrell, I didn't want him to be right. I rubbed my fingertips together. Flickers of light sparked from my hand. I needed to be ready just in case.

"Stand down," I ordered the weapons wielder. "Before it's too late."

"Too late for who?" The guy spit, then sneered at me and Farrell.

The thugs Farrell and I had leveled started groaning. "We need to take him out before they get up," Farrell warned.

A bullet discharged. It struck Farrell from behind. He stumbled forward. Spinning around, I hurled a stream of energy at a shooter who had snuck up from the rear, then lodged a blast at the bearded man in the road before he could let loose a bullet of his own. His body sailed through the air, his rifle spinning in the opposite direction. People started yelling and running. Grabbing Farrell, I brought him close, then sent a field of energy around us like a protective cocoon.

Farrell slumped to the ground, clutching his chest. Blood seeped through his fingers. White vapor poured out of his hand and into his wound as he worked to heal himself. Sweat beads dotted his forehead. "This is going to take me a minute," he groaned through clenched teeth. "And we don't have a minute."

The townies regrouped. They eyed me and Farrell with fear and shock. They circled us with raised weapons. Up on his feet now and back with his weapon, the older man in overalls hollered, "They're aliens!"

With my abilities, I could easily have leveled the crowd with a blast, but a kid no older than ten caught my eye. His hands shook as he pointed a colt revolver at us. Horror filled his eyes. To them, we were space invaders, and all they were doing was protecting their own.

"Take them out, Fleet," Farrell urged.

Seeing no other way out of our predicament, I pressed my hand against the ground. I let loose a surge of energy. The earth around us split. A deluge of soil and rocks shot up into the sky. The men were flung into the air as their weapons discharged. Out of nowhere, a green hue erupted. It blanketed the scene and halted everything in place. Bullets hovered mid-air. Bodies froze.

Colleen shimmered into view. She wound her way through the chaotic scene and came up to me and Farrell. "Seems you two could use some assistance."

Farrell clambered to his feet. Still weak from the gunshot, he leaned against me. "Not from the likes of you."

"Maybe a little," I said to Farrell. Before he could object, I touched his forehead. I sent a trickle of power into him. He slumped in my arms, and I eased him to the ground.

Dropping my shield, Colleen came forward. She eyed Farrell's nearly healed wound. She lighted her fingers on it and finished the job with her green vapor.

"Thank you, Colleen."

"You are welcome. Now, take Farrell to the cabin while I clean up this mess."

Even though I had come here wanting to contact her, I hadn't wanted to do it like this. Farrell and I were exposed. Lives were almost lost. Confident in Colleen's ability to restore the area and wipe every-one's minds, I latched onto Farrell's wrist. I pictured the Pure's cabin in my mind. Smoky gray tendrils of vapor poured out of me and swirled around my feet. Weightlessness came over me. Farrell and I trans-ported out of the town and onto the porch of Colleen's cabin. Taking in the surrounding area, I saw Max and the traveler from Texas standing by a bonfire. The traveler rushed over to me.

"Fleet!" He eyed Farrell, still out on the ground. "Man, what happened to Farrell?"

I studied his face to see if anything about him would come to me, but all I remembered was walking into camp with him and Dominique. "You know me? And my brother?"

His faced dropped. "Not you, too."

"Too?"

"Dominique doesn't remember me either."

Richard and Sue came out of the cabin. Together with Max, they carried Farrell inside and set him on the couch. Sue lifted his eyelids for inspection. "He's fine. Looks like we have about an hour before he comes to." She motioned for me and the others to gather in the kitchen. "Come, we have a lot to discuss."

Colleen appeared. "We most certainly do."

Gazing at the Pure's green eyes, noticing Trent's were blue, I wondered how he fit into the group.

"What word do you bring, Fleet?" Colleen asked.

"I bring this." Reaching into my pocket, I brought out the folded note. I opened it and read it out loud. "We are from the future. We are the Pure. We need to find Trent. Signed Dominique and myself." I tossed the parchment on the table. My attention fixed on the traveler. "Now that I have found you, I take it you can explain this."

Trent lifted the note carefully, as if it were an ancient document. He scanned the contents a few times. He turned it around and examined the other side. "This is Dominique's handwriting and her signature. I'd know it anywhere." He peered at me. "Is this your signature?"

"Yes, it is. Though, I have no recollection of signing the note. When we awoke, it was simply there."

Looking faraway, Trent halfway mumbled. "You and Dominique must've written this so you wouldn't forget."

I leaned forward. "So we wouldn't forget what?" Trent paced the room, while Colleen and the others kept their silence. "What?" I asked again, but with little patience. "Would not forget what?"

Trent handed me the paper. "That you, me and Dominique are from the future. We came to this time to stop Dominique from being marked by Tavion in order to save our future child."

A hard shudder passed through my body. *The future?* I threw Colleen a look. "Is he mad?"

"He is not," she answered.

"I don't understand," I muttered, eyeing the traveler.

"Let me start over," he offered. Taking his time, he explained our roles in the future, ending with the revelation that the three of us had come to the past to prevent Dominique from being marked by Tavion, but had inadvertently created a new timeline where almost everything was switched. "And now you and Dominique have lost your memories."

His explanation could have knocked me to my knees, but I kept as steady as possible as he answered every question I had. The idea of Dominique being marked, hunted, and killed for lifetimes by Tavion incensed me, until it dawned on me that she was now aligned with the hunters.

"Switched alliances and lost memories," I whis-

pered, grappling with the traveler's tale. "Once a
Pure, but now Tainted." The note came into view.
Dominique's signature stood out among the writing.
"Your mission has been accomplished. She will most
certainly not be marked. So now what?"

"The mission is about much more than
Dominique," Trent said. "If not her, someone else will
be marked. Lives will be lost. Innocents will still be at
risk. Plus, she's a Tainted now. I know she'd never
want to be one of them, so I still need to save her."

"And you know as well as I do that the Tainted
will never stop their campaign against humankind,"
Colleen cautioned.

Glancing at my sleeping brother, I knew Colleen
was right. The Tainted would never change their
ways. They would always hate humankind. And now
Dominique had set her sights set on wiping out the
Pures because of what they did to Tavion. They
needed to know.

Looking away from the group, overcome with the
horror of what I was about to reveal, I lowered my
voice. "She plans to kill all of you at the marking."

Sue gasped. She grasped Richard's hand. "She
cannot. We had agreed on marking one of our own."

Shaking my head, not wanting to believe it myself,
I uttered, "She is going rogue."

"But she is always kept away when we are near,"
Max blurted. "How can she strike?"

Remembering the look on Dominique's face when
she had explained her plan, I said, "She will find a
way. Trust me."

"Let her try," Colleen interjected. "We need her
there for our plan to work, anyway."

The air in the house stilled. Palpable fear covered the faces of the Pures. I raised my eyebrow. "Plan?"

Taking a gulp, the traveler started explaining how he'd be presented as the marked one. Once handed over, Colleen and the others would entangle the Tainted with energy streams while he sent his aura into the Tainted in order to expel the evil from them.

The plan sounded impossible. "I can sense you have powers, but something like that would require exponential strength."

Richard patted Trent on the back. "This young man is a Supreme."

Trent rubbed his palms on his pants. "A Supreme who doesn't exactly know how to use his abilities."

My mind processed Trent's identity and the fact that he, Dominique and I were from the future. Was it really true? As outlandish as it seemed, it would explain my absent memories. More importantly, how could Trent do what he said? I didn't know much about Supremes, let alone those who hadn't mastered their skills.

"What if your plan fails?" I asked. "Then what?"

"We fight," Colleen announced. "With everything we've got."

"And when it's all said and done," Trent added, "you, Dominique, and I will go back to our time."

Richard and Max broke into conversation about maneuvers and techniques. Sue joined them, but Colleen, Trent and I didn't. The gravity of the plan weighted us down with worry and anticipation. Eyeing the time traveler with his peculiar clothing, I gave him a slight nod, letting him know I was ready to do whatever it took to protect innocents. Even though I had no idea how the plan would unfold, I had to believe everything would work out.

Farrell moaned. The group silenced. Colleen ushered me over to where Farrell lay. "Time for you and your brother to go." She placed my hand on his. "The town has been mind-wiped. The damaged to the road is repaired. You should have no problem returning."

With my hand on Farrell's, I concentrated on the outside of the Mansion House. The beige-colored, two-story, wood plank house with a deep wrap-around porch became clear in my mind. Easing Farrell to his feet and wrapping his arm around my shoulders, I leaned him against me. I took one last look at the Pures before sending my gray mist out of me. It collected around my feet, swirling under me and Farrell like a funnel cloud. Slipping into weightlessness, Farrell and I materialized on the porch of our inn.

"What is happening?" Farrell muttered through half-opened eyelids. He looked around. "Has something happened to us?"

"I will explain after we get to our room," I grunted, shifting his weight around so I could open the door. "Can you walk?"

I released my hold, thinking he would be able to carry his own weight, but his knees buckled. Swooping in, I caught him before he could timber over. "Never mind, I got you."

Like two drunks stumbling in from a night of drinking, we half-walked, half-shuffled through the front door and up the stairs. Luckily, the evening had grown too late for anyone to be up and notice our spectacle. Propping Farrell against the wall, I stuffed my hand in my pocket and fished out the room key. With a click, we were inside. I eased Farrell onto the bed, then lit a nearby candle with a flick.

"Explain," Farrell ordered.

Gripping his boot, I gave a tug. "You were shot. I healed you, but overdid it a bit." His boot thumped to the floor. "I didn't mean to make you so groggy."

Farrell rubbed the spot where he had been shot. "I have always said you needed to improve your healing skills."

Laughing because he was right, I worked on his other boot. "Well, you are the skilled healer, and I am the skilled tracker. Perhaps we need to work on what the other can do."

"Yes," Farrell said with a grin. "For times like this."

With his boots off, I placed a knitted white blanket over him. "Sleep, Brother. We can discuss our short-comings tomorrow."

With eyes closed, he muttered, "Did you handle those ruffians?"

"Sure did." I patted him on the shoulder. "Get some rest, now."

Thinking Colleen must have added a sleeping aid while she healed Farrell, I watched as Farrell drifted back into slumber. Blowing out the candle, I sat in the dark and thought of the day's revelations. Dominique and I were from the future, and in that time we were both Pures, though not together. Instead, Dominique was with Trent and they were here to save their future child. More importantly, our fates would be decided in less than two days by a Supreme who had no idea how to harness his power. In this life, as in our future, everything would come down to the marking. I wondered if we'd survive it.

~INFINITI~

Walking with my feline companion alongside Farrell and Fleet while they rode into town for supplies, I became caught up in Farrell's explanation for why he believed the way he did.

"Do you ever long for peace, Brother?" Fleet had asked.

After a long pause, Farrell mentioned a man named Mr. Boardman who had come to Michigan and opened a saw mill. Filled with anger, Farrell blamed Boardman for changing things in the area.

"The river is named after a man who destroyed nature?" I looked from Farrell to Fleet, then back to little dude. "How disgusting."

Farrell started speaking of the atrocities against Native Americans. He mentioned tribes from the area and said they were known as the Good People. Mesmerized by his passion, I remembered studying the Trail of Tears in school and how so many Native American tribes were forced from their lands. The story brought tears to my eyes then, and brought them again now while listening to Farrell, especially since I was surrounded by their native ground.

"So awful." Eying the brush around us, the wild berries, and the new trees, I looked down at little dude. "Think of living with nature and having someone kick you out because they wanted your land."

Studying blond-haired Farrell on his horse, looking as hot as ever, I started admiring his position. Everything he'd said made perfect sense, but then I realized something. "Wait a minute, he's the bad guy. So if I'm on his side, does that make me a….?" I shuddered, unable to finish the thought that I could be anywhere near what a Tainted was. "Forget that."

Strolling alongside the brothers, I wondered how I'd ever get through to Fleet or anyone else for that matter. Trent wanted me to tell him and Dominique about his plan. As much as I wanted to, I couldn't get through to anyone. Fleet couldn't hear me, but maybe Dominique could. The last time I'd seen her, she and Fleet were in the cabin alone while the others were having their secret meeting. After that, I had floated off to find Trent. Now I had floated my way back to Fleet and had found him on this road.

"Okay," I said to little dude. "I'll keep trying with Fleet, and if that doesn't work, I'll go find Dominique."

We emerged from our grass trodden path onto a dirt road that widened as we got closer to… a town? A few simple log structures and some board ones were erected on one side of the street. A handful of people were milling about. "This is a really small town," I whistled, marveling at the scarcity of it. "Is something like this even called a town?"

Eyeing the simply dressed and somewhat dirty townspeople, I wondered what their days were like. "So, what's everyone up to?" I asked, joking around as if they could hear me. "Seen any good movies lately?"

Farrell and Fleet led the horses to a beige two-story house. It had a huge wrap-around porch. A sign hanging by the front door said Mansion House. "So, I guess y'all are staying here?" I gulped, thinking it looked like a creepy house from a scary movie. "Glad I'm already dead 'cause no way in heck would I ever stay in a place like that."

They were securing their horses to a post outside the house, when a whisper wafted my way. "Hey, you," a hushed female voice said.

Looking around, I wondered who had spoken and why the person would whisper to Farrell and Fleet. Were the brothers known around here? Did someone want to tell them something?

"You, spirit girl."

My shimmery spine tingled. My mouth fell open. I glanced at little dude. "Did you hear that?" He laid his ears back and hissed. "Oh yeah, you heard that all right."

Trying to fake being tough, I put my hands on my hips and peered about, mustering my courage. I wasn't gonna let anyone scare me. Thinking of one of my favorite movies, I called out, "I am the ghost now!" I quickly realized how stupid I sounded. "Nevermind. Who's there?"

A tall, thin woman in a black dress emerged from

behind the Mansion House. With pale skin and sunken eyes, she beckoned me with long fingers. "Come."

Doing a double take, I pointed to myself. "Me? You can see me?"

She nodded, and kept motioning me near. Spying Fleet and Farrell who were now walking away from the Mansion House and further into the town, I moved closer to the woman. "How can you see me?"

Still silent and waving for me to follow, she led me to a shack in the back. She approached the door and held it open. A board with a hand painted on it hung against the outer wall. Numbers lined the palm and each digit. "You're a palm reader?"

The woman stood to the side. "Yes, now please, enter."

Last time I had gone into a suspicious looking house, I had been ambushed and nearly murdered. I was with Dominique, Farrell, and Trent and we were in Houston in 1930. The house had belonged to Trent's ancestors. My friends and I had made it out of there, but standing here in the way way past with a creepy woman brought back all the fears from that evening. Although I was dead and a ghost, I didn't trust going into that shack. Even little dude had second thoughts and hung back.

"You are safe," the woman said with a deep voice.

Not feeling super comforted, but trusting that everything happens for a reason, I stepped into the small structure. Even though I was a ghost, cold air blanketed me. The heavy scent of dirt and wood penetrated my transparent nasal cavities. The door behind me swung closed with a whoosh. Looking around the candle-lit space, I saw the same woman sitting at a table in the middle of the room. I shrieked and whipped my head around to the woman who had ushered me in, but she was gone now.

"You are r-r-right th-there," I stammered to the seated woman. "But a second ago you were walking inside with m-m-e."

"I am here, I am there," she said. "It is of no matter." She motioned at the chair in front of me. "Please, sit."

Gathering up my ghostly courage, I told myself nothing could happen to me because I was already dead. The woman laughed. "I am, too."

"You're....dead?" My curiosity forced me to shuffle closer to the woman. I slid into the chair across from her.

"I am, though the people here are unaware. I died in a town far from here."

"Wow, really?" I started to relax in front of the woman. "Who are you anyway?"

"My name is Gertrude Kelly."

"Kelly," I repeated. "You know, I had a neighbor across the street from me named Jan Kelly. She was the coolest. She was into stuff like crystals and cards, and she was always showing me neat things about..." My words trailed off. My nerves skyrocketed. Was this ghost somehow related to Jan? I let out a nervous laugh. "You're not like connected to Jan somehow. Are you?"

"People often find themselves linked to the same souls time and time again. Some call it coincidence.

Others refer to it as fate, though it is much deeper than that."

"Oh," I said with a smile, as if I understood her. Too embarrassed to admit how confused I was, I changed the subject. "So, you know what it's like to be dead and walking around? And you can interact with living people?"

The woman smiled. "Yes and yes."

Taking a good look at her, thinking she was wearing her funeral outfit, I guessed she was probably in her eighties. Deep lines traced her pale face. She had white hair pulled back in a long ponytail. Unsure of what to say or do, I lifted my hands from my lap and placed them palm up on the table. "My body is mostly vapor, but I guess you can try to read my palms if you want. I'm totally into stuff like that."

"No palm reading for you, young one. I brought you here to remind you about yourself."

"Remind me about myself?" I wasn't sure what she meant.

She leaned forward and pressed her transparent hands on mine, as if gripping them. "You are special."

I'd often been called "special" when I was growing up by a mean girl on my street, and it struck a nerve. Though I knew she meant it in a different way, I wanted her to clarify. Slowly pulling my hands away from her, I asked, "What do you mean, special?"

She closed her eyes. "Your unearthly energy is not like any I have ever encountered." She slowly opened her eyes and tilted her head. She waved her hand in the air. "Nothing can touch you. I sense that I need to remind you of that."

I thought of being a void and how Transhuman powers had no effect on me. Was she talking about that? If so, it didn't matter because I was dead. "Well, not to state the obvious, but I am ghost, you know. Nothing can touch me. It's a perk." I laughed, but quickly stopped when I noticed her frown. "Nevermind."

The silence deepened between us. The woman probed me with her stare. Itching to leave, and about to say goodbye, she leaned in close to me. Her etched face and long nose hovered way too close for comfort. "You must use your strengths," she whispered.

Shivering with fright, I scooted away from her. I clambered to my feet before I could fall over on my airy ass. I started for the door. "Uh, okay. Thanks, but I gotta go."

The woman called out, "To speak to the living, you must call on emotion!"

Her words glued me in place. I thought of the times I had tried to communicate with Dominique, Fleet, and Trent. I was pretty sure I had used a lot of emotion. I had cried, yelled, stomped my feet. I had even done jumping jacks. I looked over my shoulder at the woman who remained seated in the window-less home, shrouded in black attire and illuminated by candlelight. I asked in a timid voice, "And if that doesn't work?"

She thought for a second. She raised her finger when something came to her. "Dreams! You can infiltrate dreams with enough concentration."

I did an awkward half-bow out of sheer nervous-ness, said another goodbye, and darted out of the tiny shack. Little dude came up and started purring and circling my feet. "Well, that was weird," I muttered to him. "Come on," I said, hurrying to the main road and back to where I saw Fleet and Farrell walking. "Let's find the boys."

Circling the area, walking up and down the empty drag, I didn't see them. I even returned to the Mansion House where their horses were tethered, and floated around the rooms. No sign of the brothers. Back outside, I slumped down on the porch. "Nothing is going my way. As usual."

The night had grown pitch dark. The stars above twinkled brightly. Only a few candles in the windows of the inn indicated anyone was still awake.

"What a boring life," I said to myself, thinking about living in this time. But then I remembered the two weeks I had endured with no electricity after a hurricane blew into Houston. I had gone to bed early every night because there was nothing to do without power. I had never been so well rested before. Then I recalled something else—sitting by candlelight with my mom, playing cards, talking about anything and everything. We had gotten so close during that time. My shimmery self started brimming with sadness. My insides filled with heart ache. I missed her so much, and would do anything to see her again. Little dude let out a melancholy cry.

"I know," I said to him, thinking he wanted to comfort me somehow. "I'll stop. This is no time for a meltdown." Standing up and telling myself to get it together, I redirected my attention. "I'm going to Dominique. Catch up with me if you can."

My slinky friend had started to wander off, probably for food or water, which was fine by me. I needed to find Dominique right away. With the advice the dead palm reader had given me about dreams, I had no doubt I'd get through to her.

Concentrating on her, I pictured her clearly in my mind—brown hair, green eyes, long legs. And then I thought of her butt. Was it big? Small? I couldn't remember, but laughed at myself for thinking of her ass. I had always hated my butt because it was flat and small. If I got out of this mess and changed my destiny so I'd be alive in the future, I vowed to do squats.

"Geez, focus," I whispered out loud, forcing my attention back on Dominique. After a few seconds, my transparent self floated into the air. My form started gliding through the sky. Quickly out of the town, I soared over the trees and brush until I found myself at the Boardman River. Following the trickling water, I ended up in front of the cabin where Fleet and Dominique had stayed the night before.

"This is where the evil people live," I whispered to myself, scanning the area to make sure no one was around.

Stepping through the log wall, I glided to the room where Dominique slept. "Hey, it's me," I whispered. An aching feeling for home and friendship swelled inside me. Lying on the bed, I faced my best friend. Long strands of hair covered her face. Her mouth parted as she breathed slow and deep. I thought of the countless sleepovers I had when I was a kid, wishing I could go back to that simpler time. Then I slapped myself. Even though my hand drifted through my face, the effect was successful. Out of my funk, I closed my eyes and thought of dreams. Fluffy clouds, rainbows, candy, Hot Cheetos, and even Root Beer. My favorite things flashed before my eyes.

As I thought of dreamlike vibes and all things calm and peaceful, a strange sensation crawled over me. Heat seared my nasal passages. Prickly needle-like pain stung my skin. Opening my eyes, I found myself in a red desert. Stranger still, I wasn't a glob of vapor anymore. I pinched my arm and tugged my hair. "Whoa, I should've done this whole dream visi-tation thing earlier."

Turning around and taking in the desolate land-scape, I spotted Dominique. Staring up at the sky, she held out her hands. Bright red blood poured from her palms, like a waterfall. "What the—?" I ran over to her. "Dominique, what are you doing?"

Keeping her gaze in place, she whispered, "He's coming to kill me."

Following her line of sight, I saw a black mist in the clouds. The churning mass of darkness barreled our way. Grabbing her shoulders, I shook her until she noticed me. "This is your dream and we need to get out of here, right the hell now!"

Her expression went from stunned to relieved. "Infiniti!"

"Yes, it's me! Now think of a peaceful place!"

"The beach!" she hollered.

With a whoosh, we found ourselves standing on sand. A salty breeze blew about us. A magnificent sun shone bright. The ocean water rippled peacefully. Dominique studied her hands for a few seconds. With no sign of blood, she dropped them to her sides.

"Are you...real?" She reached out and poked my cheek.

With my throat clogged over with tears, I managed to squeak out. "I'm a ghost and all, and we're in your dream, but yeah, it's me."

She brought me in for a desperate hug. Holding onto each other for dear life, it took us forever to part. And when we separated, we started talking at the same time. I laughed. "You first."

She drew in a deep breath and pressed her hand against her chest. "Here in my dreams I'm still me, but out in the world, out in first life, I've forgotten who I am."

Her words danced around in my head. "Huh?"

A frightened expression darkened Dominique's features. "I've lost my memories. Fleet, too. So out there in the real world, I'm one of the bad guys. Like *really* one of them. So is Fleet, except he's a traitor to the Tainted and is secretly one of the Pures." She looked down at the ground. "I can feel the hate in my heart. It's strong, and deadly, and I can't do anything about it."

My mouth fell open. "Holy shit," I whispered. "I knew about the whole bizarro world alternate reality thing, but I didn't know about the memory thing." I stopped and gazed at the ocean. "I guess I've been floating around so much I didn't catch on to you and Fleet actually melding with your selves from this time." My bottom lip started quivering. Tears trickled from my eyes. I slumped to the sandy surface. "It's all my fault."

Dominique joined me on the ground, tears welling up in her eyes, too. "No, it's not. We came here knowing the risks. If it's anyone's fault, it's the Taint-ed's. They started this whole mess."

"Those bastards," I muttered.

"Exactly," Dominique said with a smile, trying to make me feel better.

We edged closer to each other and sat shoulder to shoulder, both of us crying and lost in our thoughts. "How do you know about Fleet? About the traitor thing?" I asked.

"He remembered it right before we lost our memories. We even wrote a warning note to ourselves, though I have no idea what has happened to it." She scooped up a handful of sand and let it sift through her fingers. "I'm adrift, Infiniti. And I'm so scared."

She rested her head against mine. Together like that for a while, we sat in hopeless silence, staring at the ocean, contemplating our messed up situation. "Is there any part of you that's still you?"

"You mean back in reality? No. But here in this state, I remember everything up until the moment I lost my memories."

"That sucks," I whispered.

Stuck in dreamland where our thoughts and actions processed on slow motion, Dominique said, "Hey, what were you going to tell me?"

Snapping back to reality, I remembered my message. "Trent!"

As if she had forgotten him, she exclaimed, "Oh my God! Trent! He was taken by the Pures. How is he?"

"He's fine! But he wanted me to give you and

Fleet a message. I couldn't get through to Fleet, so that's why I'm here."

Her eyes widened with curiosity. "What is it?"

"He's going to offer himself up to be marked by the Tainted. He thinks he can use his powers to convert the Tainted and make them Pure."

Dominique clutched my arm and tugged on me. "He's going to do what? Infiniti, they'll kill him!"

"I know, he's crazy, and I have no idea how he can pull something like that off, but he's determined to complete the mission—save you, your future child, and all of mankind in the process."

She covered her face. Her shoulders shook while a fresh deluge of tears poured out of her. I rubbed her arms, waiting for her to finish. "He's the best thing that's ever happened to me, Infiniti. And I don't want to lose him."

"If anyone can do it, it's him," I assured her.

"You're right." She wiped her face with the back of her hands. "He has what it takes, and I'm gonna help him. He will not be alone."

Getting up, she brushed herself off. On my feet now too, filled with renewed hope, I hopped around with my dukes up, like a boxer. "Yeah, let's fight! I'm ready to kick ass!" But then I stopped and scratched my head. "How exactly are we gonna fight?"

A serious expression covered her face. "I have to remember who I am. If I can do that, then I know I can figure something out."

Her face started to blur. Her body lifted off the ground. "Oh no, I'm waking up!" She reached out to me as she faded away. "Infiniti, help me remember!"

Watching Dominique disintegrate out of her dream world, I wondered how on earth I could help her remember. Turning back into vapor while the beach scene crumbled around me, my experience with the dead palm reader sprang to mind. She said I could communicate with the living with enough emotion.

I huffed. I had plenty of damn emotion. "They ain't seen nothing yet."

~FLEET~

WITH OUR HORSES SADDLED WITH LUMBER, FARRELL AND I journeyed home in a relaxed state, our confrontation with the nearby locals bringing us closer together. We chatted comfortably and enjoyed each other's company. Yet every now and again, my thoughts drifted to my meeting with Colleen and the others. I believed the traveler and his tale of the future, not only because of the holes in my memories, but also because of the note in my pocket. A keen sense of being unsettled had entered me with my discovery of the note. It grew with each moment since. Since Dominique was also from the future, I had to believe a sense of unsettledness had occupied her as well. Should I somehow broach the subject with her?

Entering the camp, I studied the surroundings for any evidence of time travel abnormality, but found none. The cabins appeared normal. The horses, chickens, and cattle grazing the area showed no hint of irregularity.

Fleet dismounted his ride. "Are you looking for something?"

Before I could answer, Caris emerged from her cabin. "Welcome back. Did everything go well?"

Farrell and I had decided to keep our volatile encounter to ourselves, albeit for different reasons. The last thing I wanted was Stone's call for vengeance against a town of mostly innocents, while Farrell's concern was the marking. He desired no distraction from the preparation.

"Yes," Farrell answered quickly. "Everything went well."

Stone and Dominique came into the camp from the direction of the river. Stone's fishing rod was propped on his shoulder. Dominique's white dress was tied up at her knees. She flashed me a relieved smile, and picked up her pace. "You're back!"

"Yes, just now."

"No problems?"

Unsure of what I was looking for, I scanned her face for any hint of peculiarity. Finding none, I kissed her on the forehead. "None at all."

We untied the lumber hanging on the sides of our horses, and piled it near the bonfire. Stone took a stick from the ground and traced out the formation he wanted us to build. He drew a raised rectangular shape. "The platform will need to be about seven feet long, and three feet wide." He held out his hand to waist-level. "It will also need to be this high."

Grabbing the planks of wood, Farrell and I set them out according to Stone's wishes. Wasting no time, we retrieved our tools and started hammering away.

Stone walked around us as we worked, explaining the procedure. "We will lay the target face down. Then, Caris and I will send out an energy stream to immobilize the person and render him or her powerless."

"Her?" Dominique asked. Her face lost its color. Her eyes looked distant. Had a memory from the future filtered into her mind? Trent said she had been marked and killed eight times by Tavion. Did Stone's instructions to mark a 'her' bring back something?

"Yes," I said, wanting to stoke up her recollection if indeed something had come to her. "The person marked could be a female. Like you."

She looked at me as if seeing me for the first time, then blinked and shook her head. "Um, I am sorry. What were we talking about?"

Cutting off Stone before he could answer, focused on her only, I asked, "Dominique, are you all right?"

"Of course, I am," she said in a defensive tone. She turned her attention back to Stone. "Now, what were you saying?"

Stone picked up where he left off. "Once tethered and immobilized, I will send a blast into the person at the back of the neck." Stone approached Caris and pointed at the spot. "Right here, at the nape. The injection of Tainted energy at this spot will penetrate the person at the cellular level. The mark will be permanent, allowing us to track the target until completion of the agreed upon terms."

"Nine lifetimes," Farrell said. "Like they asked."

"Correct," Caris said. "Their chances of removing the mark are nil. We will kill the Marked One nine times over, plus any Pures who get in our way.

"For Tavion," Dominique said.

"Yes," Stone chimed in. "For Tavion."

Hammering my nail into the wood, unable to echo the same sentiment for Tavion, I kept one eye on Dominique. She had narrowed her gaze when referring to Tavion, appearing ready to battle anyone who crossed her. Knowing her deadly plan to take out Colleen and her group, I waited for her to ask to remain present during the ceremony, wondering if Stone and Caris would agree.

Finished with our platform, Farrell and I stood and eyed our handiwork.

"I'm staying for the marking," Dominique declared with force, preempting any talk of ushering her away. Her arms were crossed, her stance wide. "I will *not* be taken to the shelter."

Supporting her attendance because she needed to be present for Trent's plan to work, and because it fit in with her agenda of us striking the Pures, I chimed in. "I agree. Dominique should bear witness."

Caris examined Stone for his reaction. "Any objection?" she asked him.

He kept the stick in his hand. He tapped it against his palm while considering her request. "I see no problem with that. The Pures will be here for ceremony, not for battle."

With that detail out of the way, now all I had to worry about was Trent pulling off his plan before Dominique could initiate hers. Everything was up to him now, and I was prepared to do anything I could to help him be successful.

Stone gestured as he finished explaining how the procedure would occur. "Fleet and Farrell, you will light the torches as usual. For our protection, and theirs, the Pures will stay out of the ring. Only their chosen one will enter our circle. Once inside, I will perform the procedure. Understood?"

"Understood," we said together.

Farrell and I lifted our newly built platform and placed it in the center of the circular area not far from the spot for our bonfire. When we shifted the heavy piece, a cat sprang out from the nearby brush. It dashed toward Dominique and circled her feet.

"Hey," Farrell said to me with a curious expression. "It's your friend. I told you it would make a nice pet for you and Dominique."

Dominique squatted down to pet the feline. "What a lovely creature!"

I thought the cat's appearance on the road and now again at our camp strange. Eyeing the cat, I wondered if its arrival was more than happenstance. Was this the sign I had been looking for? After a long pat by Dominique, it moved over to me and circled my legs next, then rotated back and forth between us. "Seems the creature indeed wants to be our pet. What do you think, Dominique?"

Scratching the cat between the ears, she smiled "Why not?"

Her smile reminded me of a normalcy I longed for. Seeing her like that convinced me to say something to her. With the marking in one day, I had to try and get through to her. After Stone and Caris finished their instructions, I took Dominique's hand. "How about we go on a walk?"

Leaving the group, we strolled down to the river and followed the stream. The gray day carried a somber tone. Thick clouds smothered the sun. With no warmth from the sky, the chilled air hung thick around us, like an invisible wet blanket. I struggled to find the right words to begin a conversation about us being from the future. There was no way I was the only one feeling as if things were off.

Before I could say anything, she broke the silence. She stopped and turned to face me. She lifted her hand. "Do you remember giving me this ring?"

A thin silver ring with two adjoining hearts circled the ring finger of her right hand. Had I given her the ring and forgotten? Or maybe the token was from the future? From Trent perhaps? I brushed the band with my thumb. No matter its origin, I counted it as another sign. "I have no recollection of this ring." Meeting her curious gaze, I asked, "When did you notice this?"

"Yesterday morning, when we awoke. I wanted to ask you about it, but the day got away from me. And then you left for town." She eyed the ring. "It's so strange though, because I recall explaining to Caris that you had given it to me, though the exchange is missing from my memory."

She *was* experiencing weirdness like me, and the timing was the same—yesterday morning. The gray cat at our feet started purring wildly, prancing about with fervor. I eyed the creature, wondering what had riled it like that. Another sign? I needed to act.

Taking Dominique's arms, I drew her in close. "I need to tell you something."

A blast of light shot up in the sky. It burst into an array of green sparkles, then disintegrated as it tumbled back down to the earth.

"The Pures," Dominique said with alarm. "They're early." She tried to wrench away from my grasp, but I held her firm.

"Wait," I pleaded, holding onto her. "I need to talk to you."

"We need to go, Fleet."

"Not yet," I said, keeping a hold on her.

She slammed her hands against my chest and shoved me back. "What is wrong with you?"

My brain scrambled. The Pures were early, and I had not yet told Dominique about us being from the future. With no time for a lengthy explanation, I decided to change my tactic. "Do you love me?"

Taken aback, it took her a few seconds to answer. "You know I do."

"Then please," I pleaded. "I need to tell you something, and I need you to believe me."

She eyed the dying embers of the green flare. Looking eager to take off for the others, she reluctantly stayed instead. "What is it?"

The cold air gusted. Her dress flapped in the wind. Her hair blew in her face. She tucked the strands behind her ears. "Dominique, you cannot attack them."

My request sent a stormy rage into her eyes. Her fists clenched at her sides. "I knew you would not support me."

Her words cut me deep. "I am supporting you, Dominique. The real you. You know something is not right. I can tell, and I feel it too." I fished the note out of my pocket and handed it to her. "And this is why."

She read it, but the text did not change her expression. In fact, the words on the parchment multiplied her anger. She curled her lip. "You are one of them? And will go to such trickery to get me to change sides?" She crumpled the note and threw it to the ground. "The only thing not right is YOU! How dare you!"

"Dominique, it is no trickery!"

She blasted me with a charge so fierce I thought I would rip in two. My insides burned liked lava. Every molecule of my being exploded with pain. A second blast tore through me, and my vision faded to black.

~DOMINIQUE~

STARING AT FLEET WITH HIS BODY CONTORTED IN PAIN, I leveled him with another charge so he would pass out. In a rush so I could hurry back to the others, I tied him up with my energy stream, lifted him off the ground with my power, and hid him amidst a cluster of bushes.

Studying his still breathing form, horror over who he was and what I had done seeped into me. I pulled at the fabric of my dress over my chest and clenched it. I fell to my knees. Hot tears stung my eyes. "How could you do this to me, Fleet? How could you betray me? I was ready to run away with you."

Uncertainty consumed me. How could I have not known who Fleet really was? Everything about him and us had been a horrible lie. Everything. My heart shattered into a hundred thousand pieces, pieces I'd never be able to mend. Uncontrollable sobs shook my body. My new pet approached slowly. It hissed at me, and then rubbed its head against my side. "He is the enemy, not me. He brought this on himself."

Convincing myself I had done the right thing, I rubbed my face with my sleeves. Did Fleet even love me? And how long had he been with the other side? I got up slowly, telling myself it did not matter. The Pures had killed Tavion, and I was going to avenge him no matter what. I smoothed out my dress. Fleet had chosen the wrong side, and as much as it pained me, I knew I would have to come back and kill him. But first, I needed to get to the others.

Running back to the camp, I saw Father and Farrell lighting the torches. Mother spotted me right away. "Dominique," she sighed with relief. "I was about to go looking for you." She craned her neck. "Where is Fleet?"

Not wanting to detract from our preparations, and already deciding to keep Fleet's betrayal to myself and take him out later as peacefully as possible, I searched for an excuse for his absence. "We were walking when he remembered he needed something from town."

Father frowned. "He has gone to town?"

Farrell approached. He eyed me with distrust. "What? Fleet has gone to town without telling me?"

I knew I could easily deceive Mother and Father, but Farrell was different. He and his brother were close. If Fleet had gone to town, he would have said something to Farrell. "Yes. He said he forgot something and would be right back. He told me to tell you not to worry."

Eyeing Farrell with the same intensity he gave me, determined not to waver under his scrutiny, I wondered if he was a traitor, too.

"Never mind that for now," Mother said. "They are here."

The pounding of hooves echoed in the cold, misty air. The breaking of twigs and rustling of leaves sounded. Colleen and her group approached with speed. They slowed their horses when they neared and stopped outside our protective barrier. Farrell redirected his attention to our unexpected visitors, but kept close to me.

Father raised his hand at the group. "Hail, Colleen. Your arrival is premature. Or is your presence here related to something else?"

I studied the faces of my enemies—Colleen, Richard, Sue, and Max. And then my gaze settled on Trent, the traveler from Texas. Colleen had infiltrated our camp and taken him from us, and it appeared he was now one of them. Everything seemed different after he arrived. Insurmountable anger ignited inside of me. They had killed Tavion. They had turned Fleet against me. They were as good as dead, beginning with the mysterious traveler.

"We have decided which of us will be marked," Colleen explained. "To that end, and not wanting to delay the inevitable, we are here for the ceremony. Is that acceptable?"

The fire from the torches crackled while Father considered the request. "Let me consult with my people."

With a nod from Colleen, Father turned to confer with us. He lowered his voice. "What do you all think? We are indeed ready, though missing Fleet."

"We do it," I insisted, antsy and on edge on the

inside, but trying to remain calm on the outside. "They are here and we are prepared. Why delay?"

"No," Farrell interjected. "We do this with all of us or none of us."

Right then I knew Farrell was with Fleet. It was the only thing that made sense. Maybe the early arrival by the Pures was really a plan to attack. If so, I had already taken out one of their strongest. I could easily take out the others.

"Fleet would not want us to delay," I urged, doing my best to discredit Farrell's position. "I know him better than anyone. He would say to go forward."

Farrell's jaw clenched. "I know Fleet equally as well, and I do not believe he would say that. We need to wait."

"This is a ceremony," I scoffed, trying to bolster my argument. "Not a battle." *Not yet anyway.* "You said so yourself, Father."

Father placed his hand on his chin "I most certainly did say that. Today or tomorrow. It is all the same. The sooner we can mark their chosen one, the sooner we can have our vengeance. I see no reason to delay. Caris? What say you?"

Mother blew out a breath. "Agreed."

Satisfied with the decision, and ready to kill Colleen and her followers, I stayed close to Farrell so I could blast him if he got in my way.

Mother and Father stepped toward the group. "We are amenable to your request," Father announced. "Your chosen one may enter our barrier. The rest of you must remain outside."

The Pures dismounted their steeds. As I studied them with keen interest, a dark object flashed in the corner of my eye. It was the gray cat, strolling over from the direction of the river. My heart skipped a beat. My palms grew sweaty. Had Fleet undone his binds? Was he coming for me?

Farrell raised a brow at me. He scanned the space around us and saw the cat. His line of sight extended to the path toward the river. He glowered at me. "What have you done?"

Raising my chin slightly I said, "Nothing."

The Pures formed a huddle. A quick discussion ensued. After a few seconds, the group broke apart. Colleen and the traveler stepped forward. "Where is Fleet?" Colleen asked.

My blood boiled. They turned one of ours against us, and now they wanted to know where he was?

"His whereabouts are none of your concern," Father declared with irritation in his voice. "Present the person to be marked, or leave."

Rubbing my fingers together, I wondered who they had chosen. Analyzing each face in turn, I thought it would be Max. I pictured him volunteering so his parents wouldn't have to. But to my shock, Trent stepped forward. He raised his hand slightly. "That would be me."

"No," Father objected. "He is not connected to our conflict. He is not even a Pure!"

"He most certainly is," Colleen retorted. "As for the conflict, he is deeply rooted in it. You may see for yourself."

"This is a trick," I whispered to my parents. "Do not listen to them."

"I agree," Farrell added. "This is not right."

Surprised at Farrell's agreement, I waited for

Father to respond. He silenced us with a wave and motioned for Trent to approach. "Come forth."

A shadowy, petite figure materialized next to the traveler as he moved forward. It disappeared in a blink. Catching my breath, I looked around to see if anyone else noticed the phenomenon, but no one gave any sign.

I shook it off, telling myself I was imagining things, and watched the so-called Pure advance. For the first time I noticed his striking good looks. Lean and slender with sun-kissed skin and brown hair that hung slightly in his magnetic blue eyes, I wondered where he had come from. Dressed in oddly tight-fitting clothes and wearing dark shoes with white stripes down the sides, he did not look like any Texan I had ever seen. He moved through the electrified circular field with a sizzle. He kept his stare on me, but addressed my parents. "My name is Trent Avila. I'm a Pure, and I'm ready to be marked."

Mother approached. She placed her hand on his forehead and closed her eyes. Her metallic-colored mist swirled out of her hands and oozed onto his skin. She gasped. She jerked her hand back. "He is a Supreme!"

"Protect Dominique!" Father yelled.

The Pures charged. Blasts whizzed about me. Farrell pushed me to the ground. He covered my body as an array of colors lit up around us and electrical sparks rained down like a fiery war. The ground shook. Vibrations rocked my head and ears. And then, everything stopped.

Farrell scrambled to his feet. He helped me up. The scene before us could not have been worse.

Mother and Father were tied in strands of multi-colored, crackling energy binds. Their mouths were gagged. Richard, Sue, and Max stood over them, directing beams at their heads.

Colleen and the traveler approached me and Farrell. The tall leader of the Pures carried her ignited staff. A hazy blue vapor hugged the traveler, making him look supercharged and deadly.

"One wrong move and you will force us to obliterate your people," Colleen warned. "Now, where is Fleet?"

Farrell formed a deadly ball of electricity in his palm. I formed one of my own. "Why such a keen interest in my brother?" Farrell asked through gritted teeth.

Trent stepped in front of Colleen. "He's not from this time, Farrell. Neither is Dominique and neither am I. The three of us are from the future. We should've never come here and we need to get back. Now please, where is he?"

"Lies," I spat. "Do not believe them, Farrell. Fleet is one of them, and they have concocted a fairy tale to hide the truth."

My parents and Stone writhed when they heard my claim. Even Farrell's light flickered as he considered my assertion that Fleet was a traitor.

"Dominique," the traveler pleaded, edging closer to me. "It's true, we're not from here. I know you can feel it. Now, where is he?"

Glaring at him, I lied. "I killed him when I found out he was a traitor."

The ball in Farrell's palm collapsed. Shock filled his eyes. "You did what?"

The shadowy figure appeared again. This time her image held, allowing me to see her small features and big hair. "Dominique, can you see me? Dear baby Jesus, tell me you can see me!"

I looked at the others, wondering if they could see the spirit girl too, but they gave no indication.

Her eyes widened when she realized I could indeed see her. She fumbled out her words in rapid fire succession. "It's me! Infiniti! Trent is your boyfriend. You love him. We are from the future. For real. Me, you and Fleet. You have to listen to Trent, he's gonna save y'all. Oh, and Fleet, I saw him take off those energy whatever thingys, and he's coming to help you! He should be here any— "

"STOP!" I whisked the girl away with my stream of power.

Everyone looked at me like I was crazy, and maybe I was, but I refused to be fooled by tricks of illusion. Farrell distanced himself from me. He fired up his weapons, fashioning two fresh orbs in his hands. He aimed one at me and the other at Colleen and Trent.

Colleen whispered something to the traveler. She backed away. The traveler inched closer to me, unfazed by Colleen's retreat and Farrell's threatening display. "You saw Infiniti, didn't you? The petite girl with big hair? She's your best friend, Dominique. She died for you. She took her last breath in your arms in the future, where we're from."

Staring into his sapphire eyes, searching for a hint of recognition, I found none. Holding my head high, ignoring his absurd claims, I snapped, "You're dead."

"Stop!" Fleet hollered.

Fleet bolted in my direction. I swept my arms wide, powering up to strike him and the traveler simultaneously, when the traveler charged into me. He wrapped his arms around me and held on tight. "Get back!" he yelled at Fleet.

With a look of confusion on his face, Fleet slowed down. He dashed over to Farrell instead. The energy flares in Farrell's hands broke apart as he united with his brother.

The traveler kept his hold. "I love you, Dominique, and we're going home. But first, I'm going to rid you and your people of the evil inside of you. Colleen!" he hollered. "Bring them over here! Fleet, get Farrell!"

I could hear Colleen shouting orders to her people to bring my parents closer. Farrell and Fleet launched into their own lightning battle. Jerking my arms, and pulling with all my might, I seethed, "Let me go!"

The traveler's body pressed against mine in a deadly embrace. Our faces nearly touched. He whispered, "You know me, Dominique. Better than anyone. You have to remember."

Know him? Impossible! Fiery strength and wild anger coursed through my veins. Heat raked at my skin. Crackles of lightning cascaded out of me. I pushed my energy out of me, hell-bent on killing my new enemy.

The traveler blocked my efforts with ease, multiplying the sapphire hue around his body. It poured out of him like a tidal wave, casting a deep shade around the area. The color had no start and no finish. It was as if we had been plunged into a deep blue ocean. "Dominique, stop fighting me."

"Now, Trent Avila!" Colleen hollered. "Do it now!"

Determined to overpower him before he could do whatever it was they had planned, I gnashed my teeth. I focused on directing my superconductor strength at him, pushing with all my might. A deep rumble vibrated inside of me. Unimaginable force brimmed at my core.

"STOP!" a symphony of voices hollered. A vanilla scent wafted my way. A host of spirits materialized— the girl the traveler had called Infiniti, a small child with long, white hair, an older, tall woman with deep wrinkles. There was even a woman with tan colored skin, long dark hair, and piercing blue eyes. She bore a striking resemblance to the traveler. They circled me and my enemy, blocking out everyone else.

"*No estás solo, Trenius,*" the woman with blue eyes said.

"*Ayúdame,*" he pleaded. "All of you, please, help me."

Ignoring the phantom figures, I continued channeling my strength into the traveler until a brilliant white flash burst out of me. It held strong, growing with enough intensity to overtake the ocean-like atmosphere. His mouth parted with intense pain. His form started wavering. A lone tear traveled down his cheek. He brought his face closer to mine. "I will always be there for you, Dominique. When things are good and when things are bad. No matter what we may face, both now and in the future. I will love you until the day I die." He pressed his lips against mine as he started disintegrating.

~TRENT~

LOCKING DOMINIQUE IN MY EMBRACE, CONCENTRATING on my aura, I pushed it out of me until it bathed everything in blue. "Stop fighting me," I pleaded. Marveling at her strength and determination to kill me, I wondered how long I could keep her from completing her task and whether I could perform the *limpia* on her and the others while holding onto her. Ridding her of her Tainted energy was my only hope for survival.

Glancing over her shoulder, I saw Colleen and the others struggling to bring Caris and Stone closer to me. Not far from them were Fleet and Farrell, embroiled in their own battle.

Trapped in a deadly hold with the woman I loved, and with Fleet and Farrell too far away from me, I didn't think I could do the ritual, let alone survive this moment. Dominique gritted her teeth with effort, when I detected a vanilla scent. A low vibrating hum filled my ears.

"STOP!" a choir of voices hollered.

Infiniti materialized, followed by Abigail, Jan, and my mom. The last time I had seen her was when I was eight. She had kissed me on the forehead, ushered me to the school bus, and later that day died in a car crash along with my dad. My heart swelled with love and heartache. She gave me a look, as if telling me everything would be okay, but I didn't think it possible. "*No estás solo, Trenius.*"

I'm not alone. Those three words reassured me, filtering hope through my veins. She had been with me this whole time, comforting me while I was here. She and the others had to be able to help me. They just had to. "*Ayúdame.* All of you, please, help me."

Dominique's light burst out of her like a nuclear weapon. It swathed my aura, overcoming it with ease. The sensation of a million stab wounds pounded my body. I wanted to cry out, but I couldn't make a sound. It felt as if my body was melting from the inside out.

My eyes watered. A tear fell down my face. Studying Dominique and the sprinkle of freckles that dotted her nose and cheeks, I still loved her. The vow I made to her when I had given her the promise ring came to mind. I repeated the words, desperate to stir in her some sort of recollection about our love for each other. Yet she continued with her attack. I pressed my lips against hers as the feeling of drifting into the wind swept over me.

"I am a void! Nothing can touch me!" a small voice cried out.

"*Ayúdale! Pronto!*" another voice begged.

The sensation of a cool breeze budded inside of me. It grew quickly, filtering its way from the center of my being to my furthest extremities, like a welcomed cold front on a blistering day. No longer coming apart, my body started to mend.

"What's happening?" I asked myself.

"It's me, Infiniti. Thanks to the ghost lady I met earlier, I remembered I'm a void and I'm inside of you now. Dominique can't touch you while I'm here. Now do your Mexican mojo on those Tainted assholes and let's end this and get out of here!"

Staring at me in surprise, Dominique realized her attempt to kill me was failing. Shocked, she uttered, "It's not possible."

"With love, anything is possible," I explained, still holding her to me.

"Damn straight," Infiniti said from within me.

Closing my eyes, I focused on Dominique, Farrell, Stone and Caris. I pictured them in my mind. I blew out, and whispered, *"Limpia."* My aura swirled out of me. I sensed it reaching out, lacing the Tainted, penetrating them from head to toe. My light became a part of them. It beat with their hearts, it breathed with their lungs. It overrode their internal struggle until it forced the evil out of them.

A hush fell down on us.

Dominique broke the silence. "What did you do?"

Opening my eyes, I saw her faced had relaxed. Her tensed body had eased. Confusion painted her expression along with a softness I hadn't seen since we arrived here. "What did you do to me?"

Infiniti's ghostly form stepped out of me, and joined the others. "You did it!" Infiniti exclaimed.

"Mi hermoso hijo," my mom said. She caressed my face with her translucent touch. *"Te amo."* The shim-

mery bodies of my mother, Jan, and Abigail faded. Infiniti remained and stayed by my side.

Taking everything in, I saw Colleen had released Stone and Caris's binds. Looking as if they had awakened from a dream, they held on to each other, gazing about with wonder. They started to approach Dominique, but Colleen blocked them with her staff. "Let the traveler finish."

"I'm going to let you go now," I said to Dominique. "Nice and slow."

Still in a state of bewilderment, she whispered her assent. I released my hold. She stepped away from me and studied her hands. "What am I feeling?"

"You are feeling what it's like to be a Pure," Colleen explained. "All of you are, thanks to Trent Avila."

Fleet, together with Farrell, approached with caution. Everyone circled around me now. Relieved and surprised the *limpia* worked, it was time to get home. I prayed my luck would hold.

"Well," I said, clearing my throat. "With that done, it's time for me, Dominique and Fleet to return to our proper time. If I'm right, the three of us will leave here, but the part of Dominique and Fleet that's from here will remain. Once separated, everyone's memories should be restored."

Dominique darted to her parents and hugged them tight. Fleet clasped his brother on the shoulder. After their quick goodbyes, and putting their faith in me, Fleet Dominique, and I clasped hands.

"I am so sorry, Fleet," Dominique blurted.

"I am, too," he said.

With no time to lose, I shut my eyes tight. "Go back to where we came from," I said. Fleet repeated my words, as did Dominique. Even Infiniti chimed in. The four of us chanted the phrase in unison over and over and over.

My mind filled with images of *Abuela's* house—white picket fence, small antique furnishings, a buttery yellow painted kitchen with avocado green appliances, a wall of crosses with a portrait of Jesus in the middle. The home came into sharp focus. I could even smell *Abuela's* enchiladas cooking in the oven. "Go there," I whispered.

Swirling vapor whipped around me. The ground dropped from beneath my feet. We plunged into nothingness. Feeling Dominique and Fleet's hands, but unable to see their bodies, we soared through darkness. Images started flashing all around me. I saw different landscapes—mountains, rivers, beaches, cityscapes. Through each terrain, I caught glimpses of people, too—Richard and Sue fishing, Caris and Stone on an airplane, Max walking down the hallway of a school. I even saw Farrell and Fleet sitting by a bonfire. As I soared through lifetimes and places, the landscapes blurred together, until everything shone as bright as the sun.

DASHING AROUND MY ROOM, I OPENED MY CLOSET ONE last time to make sure I wasn't forgetting anything. "*Mijo*, you'll only be forty-five minutes away. If you forget something, you can come get it."

I knew she was right, but I didn't want to forget

something I might need my first week of college. "I know, *Abuela*," I laughed. "You're right, as usual."

She crossed her arms and smiled. "*Como siempre.*"

Mom came into the room with a box in her hands. "I found another box!"

I took it from her and tossed it on my bed. "Thanks, Mom!"

Placing my shoes and backpack in the box, I folded the top closed and taped it up. I dusted off my hands. I looked around my empty room. "I think that's it."

Mom rested her hand on my shoulder. "Your dad is looking down on you right now with the biggest smile on his face." Her eyes watered. Tears started falling down her face. I brought her in for a hug so she wouldn't see my own emotional display. Dad died in a car crash when I was eight. I missed him every single day. I knew Mom and *Abuela* did, too.

"It going to be okay, Mom."

The sound of a horn honking out front jarred us back to reality. Mom and I separated slowly. "I bet that's Julio," she said. Forcing herself to be strong she added, "Let's get you out of here."

"*Claro,*" *Abuela* added, pulling the dishtowel from her shoulder and giving me a playful swat. "*Necesitas ir.*"

She was right. I needed to go before anyone else broke down in tears. "Okay, okay. Sheesh," I laughed. "I'm going."

Picking up the last box, I carried it to the front door. We let Julio in, and after a series of hugs, we loaded up his truck. As we stood outside, saying another round of goodbye's complete with more hugging, Infiniti screeched down the street in her Mom's sedan.

My mom shielded her eyes from the bright August sun and eyed the car. "That girl needs to watch her speed," she said with a disapproving look.

Abuela looked up with her cloudy eyes. She may have been unable to see, but she didn't need to. Infiniti's presence was always announced with fast tires and thumping bass from her car. *Abuela* shook her head. "*Aye*, Infiniti."

She parked across the street and jogged over to us. She was wearing her usual short shorts, cropped top, and cowboy boots. "Hey, *Abuela*! Hey, Mrs. A!" She gave them hugs, then smiled wide at me. She punched me on the shoulder. "I'm so glad I didn't miss you." She handed me a yellow bag with yellow tissue paper. "I got you a little something."

Happy to see one of my oldest friends, I punched her back. "Fin, you didn't have to."

She smacked her gum. "I know."

I pulled out the tissue paper to reveal a bag full of number two pencils. I laughed because I had spent all of high school bumming pencils off her.

"I figured I'd load you up with pencils since I won't be around."

"Come here, you," I said, bringing her in for a hug. Then I rubbed the top of her head, for old times sake.

"Hey," she complained. "Not the hair. I've got a lunch date with Billy."

"What?" I chuckled. "After all this time of liking him you've finally got a date...and you're both leaving for college? Good timing."

"I know, but if it's meant to be, it'll be," she shrugged. She gave me another quick hug, and started back for her car. "See you Thanksgiving, Dude. Bye, *Abuela*, bye Mrs. A!"

"That girl," Mom laughed.

After Julio and I repeated yet another round of goodbye hugs with Mom and *Abuela*, I climbed into my car. I gave my house a last look, and followed Julio across town and to Rice. Even though I was in the same city and a mere forty-five minutes away from my home, I still felt worlds away when I walked onto campus. Eyeing the magnificent arch that led to the main quadrangle, I thought of my dad, grandfather, and great-grandfather, and how they had been groundskeepers here. A lump formed in my throat. Looking up at the sky, I thought of them and placed my hand over my heart. My being here was about more than just me.

"Hey, *Primo*. You know where you're going?" Julio stood beside me with a cart stacked high with boxes. Families with their own boxes were criss-crossing all around us.

"Yeah," I said, not realizing I had stopped in place. Scanning the buildings and catching my bearings, I said, "Sorry, right over here."

Trying to pay attention to him, I turned a corner and ran into a gorgeous girl with long brown hair. I bumped into her so hard a stack of books tumbled from her arms. "Oh, man, I'm so sorry. I didn't see you."

"It's okay. I didn't see you either." The sun on her face revealed deep green eyes and a light sprinkle of freckles on her nose and cheeks. We bent over at the same time to pick up her things and knocked heads.

"Ouch," she said with a laugh, rubbing her forehead.

"Man, I'm a klutz today," I said with a pathetic smile. I held up my hands, motioning for her to stay in place. "Let me get your stuff, please. You stay right there."

I picked up her textbooks and placed them in her arms. My hands brushed against her skin. A shock exploded at our touch. A wave of tingles swept across my head and moved down the back of my neck. Staring at her, an overwhelming sense of déjà vu and familiarity came over me. It was as if I had met her before, had shared deep experiences with her, though I knew I hadn't. By the look on her face, she felt the same thing, too.

Her lips parted slightly. "Whoa."

My stomach dipped. My hands grew sweaty. "You felt that?"

"Yeah, I did." She shifted the books in her arms. "That was so…weird."

Julio coughed. "*Primo*, my arms are killing me."

A nervous laugh escaped my lips, yet I found it impossible to take my gaze away from the beautiful girl before me. "I'm Trent, this is my cousin Julio. I'm moving in today."

"I'm Dominique. I'm moving in, too." She started walking away from me, though I could tell she didn't want to. "Maybe I'll see you around?"

"Yeah, I'll look for you."

I couldn't move. I couldn't speak. I could barely breathe. All I could do was think about the feeling that coursed through me when I touched Dominique, a feeling I couldn't exactly name.

Julio waved his hand in front of my face. "Did I just witness love at first sight?"

Love at first sight? Was that it? Something inside of me stirred. A knowing. A longing. Something wonderful and indescribable. I turned to watch Dominique walking away and smiled. "I think so."

The End

NOTE FROM THE AUTHOR:

Thank you so much for taking the time to read *First Life*! If you enjoyed the story, I would appreciate it if you would help others enjoy this book, too.

Lend it. This e-book is lending enabled, so please share it with a friend.

Recommend it. Please tell other readers why you liked this book! Word-of-mouth goes a long way! You can also recommend it at your favorite e-retailer and/or review site.

Review it. Long or short and sweet, every review counts! Please tell other readers why you liked this book by reviewing it at your favorite e-retailer and/or review site.

If you do write a review, please email me at rose@rosegarciabooks.com. I'd like to personally thank you!

Once again, thanks for reading *First Life*! To stay in the know regarding my appearances and future releases, please subscribe to my newsletter at:

www.rosegarciabooks.com/newsletter.

You'll also be able to access some deleted scenes from *Final Life* when you sign up! And for those active on social media, you can find all my social media links at the bottom of each page of my website:

www.rosegarciabooks.com.

I'd love to stay in touch!

ABOUT THE AUTHOR

Rose Garcia is a lawyer turned writer who's always been fascinated by science fiction and fantasy. From a very young age, she often had her nose buried in books about other-worlds, fantastical creatures, and life and death situations. More recently she's been intrigued by a blend of science fiction and reality, and the idea that some supernatural events are, indeed, very real. Fueled by her imagination, she created The Final Life Series—a series of books about people who can manipulate the energy in and around them. Rose's books feature gut-wrenching emotional turmoil and heart-stopping action. Rose is known for bringing richly diverse characters to life as she draws on her own cultural experiences. Rose lives in Houston with her husband and two kids. You can visit Rose at: www.rosegarciabooks.com

Made in the USA
Lexington, KY
06 May 2018